I0618359

The Iron Tide

Frederick Barnes

Published by Frederick Barnes, 2025.

This is a work of fiction. Similarities to real people, places, or events are entirely coincidental.

THE IRON TIDE

First edition. December 18, 2025.

Written by Frederick Barnes.

Table of Contents

THE IRON TIDE

A Novel by Fred Barnes

PROLOGUE: THE CHATHAM ISLANDS

T he wind screams across the Chatham Islands like a wounded animal, carrying with it the salt-spray of the Pacific and secrets older than memory itself. Uncle Dread sits on his deck, carved from ancient rimu wood, watching the sun bleed into the horizon. His face is a map of violence, scarred, weathered, beautiful in its brutality. At eighty-three, he is more myth than man, descended from the Moriori who once called this isolated rock home.

His phone buzzes. Not the smartphone the young ones use. This is old school, encrypted, untraceable, a relic that connects him to an empire spanning two islands and reaching its tentacles across the Pacific.

"Uncle." The voice belongs to Rangi "Reaper" Te Kani, one of his most trusted lieutenants on the mainland.

"Speak."

"We've got a problem. The Crimson Serpents are making moves on our Shop 'n' Save contracts in Christchurch. They hit three of our collectors last night. One of them was Marcus's nephew."

Uncle Dread closes his eyes. Marcus "Sledge" Rawiri. A family man. The kind of soldier every organization needs, loyal, clean, keeps the work separate from his kids. The nephew was just a courier.

"How old was the boy?"

"Nineteen."

Silence stretches between them like the ocean between the Chathams and the mainland. Finally, Uncle Dread speaks, his voice soft as falling ash: "Send the Phantoms."

Reaper hesitates. "All four?"

"Especially Jesper, The Tasmanian Devil, let him off his leash."

The line goes dead. Uncle Dread returns his gaze to the horizon, where albatross wheel against the darkening sky. The Iron Tide has ruled New Zealand's underworld for forty years, ever since he unified the scattered gangs into one unstoppable force. They don't deal drugs, that's messy, draws too much heat. No, they're smarter. Protection rackets across every major supermarket chain, vape shops, liquor stores. They control the unions in forestry and road works, have their fingers in Fonterra dairy farms, mining operations, and DOC contracts. And Parliament? The Beehive belongs to them, majority shares hidden behind trusts and shell companies.

But empires require blood to maintain. And the Crimson Serpents have just declared war!

Uncle Dread stands, his joints cracking like gunfire. Inside his home, he opens a drawer and removes a photograph from 1987. Four young men on hand rebuilt, highly modified motorcycles. A Vincent Black shadow, Kawasaki GPZ900 Ninja, Suzuki Gsxr750 and a RG500 Gamma, each gleaming in the Auckland sun all tuned and running larger cubic capacity engines, producing even more raw torque to the back wheels. The original Phantoms. Three are dead now. The fourth still leads them.

"Time to remind them," he whispers to the ghosts, "who owns this country."

CHAPTER ONE: THE PHANTOMS

The Suzuki Hayabusa screams down State Highway 1, at 297 kilometers per hour, its rider crouched low against the wind. At this speed, the countryside blurs into impressionist smears, green farmland, white sheep, the Southern Alps rising like jagged teeth in the distance.

Jackson "Ghost" Kowalski doesn't feel fear at this velocity. He feels *alive*.

His comms crackle. "Ghost, you're going to get us all pinched before we even reach Christchurch." The voice belongs to Marcus "Sledge" Rawiri, riding the Kawasaki ZX-14R behind him, steady and controlled. That's Marcus, a balance point. Father of three. Coaches his daughter's netball team. Never brings the work home, never lets the darkness touch his family.

"Relax, Sledge," Ghost laughs into his helmet mic. "Pigs can't catch what they can't see."

"Uncle didn't send us south to get arrested for speeding violations," comes another voice. This one lacks humor entirely. Victor "Apex" Drummond, on his murdered-out Ducati Panigale V4. Ex-military. Precision instruments and cold calculation. The man you learn to despise, then realize you've been wrong about. Everyone thinks Apex is the killer. The stone-cold executioner. They're half right.

"Where's Jester?" Sledge asks.

As if summoned, Tommy "Jester" Finch pulls alongside on his neon-green Kawasaki ZX-10R, sitting *backwards* on his seat, filming himself with a GoPro.

"What's up, YouTube! Jester here, doing a hundred and eighty klicks backward! Who else is this insane? Nobody, that's who! Like and subscribe"

"Jester!" All three other Phantoms scream simultaneously.

Tommy flips forward, cackling like a madman. "Had you going! You should see your faces in my mirrors!"

"You're going to die doing something stupid," Apex says flatly.

"Yeah, but I'll die famous!"

This is the Iron Tide's elite enforcement unit. Four men on the fastest bikes in the world. When Uncle Dread wants a message sent, he sends the Phantoms. They've operated together for six years, and before that, Ghost and Apex served together in Afghanistan, though nobody talks about what happened there.

The highway curves around Lake Pukaki, its turquoise waters impossibly bright against the black volcanic soil. Tourist cars pull over as the bikes roar past in formation. This is their country. Every kilometer belongs to the Iron Tide.

Ghost's phone pings with coordinates. He slows, relatively, to 180 kph and reads the message.

Crimson Serpents HQ. The Warehouse Distribution Center, Hornby. Eighteen targets. Make it loud.

"We've got our address," Ghost announces. "Hornby industrial district. Warehouse depot."

"How many?" Sledge asks, and there's something in his voice. Not fear. Calculation. He's thinking about his nephew's body in the morgue.

"Eighteen."

Jester whoops. "Christmas came early!"

"This isn't a game," Sledge says quietly. "They killed a kid."

Silence falls over the comms, broken only by the scream of engines and wind.

"Marcus is right," Ghost finally says. "We do this clean. In and out. Send the message Uncle wants to send."

"What message is that?" Jester asks.

Apex answers, his voice like gravel scraping bone: "That the Iron Tide doesn't forget. And we don't forgive."

They blast past Timaru as the sun sets behind the mountains, painting the sky in shades of blood and bruises. Christchurch lies ahead, 200 kilometers north. The Phantoms accelerate in unison, four shadows racing toward violence.

The Hornby district sleeps under halogen lights, all industrial parks and transport depots. The Warehouse distribution center sprawls across ten acres, its red and yellow signage like a cheerful lie. During the day, it processes millions in retail goods. At night, it belongs to the Crimson Serpents.

The Phantoms park their bikes three blocks away, in the shadow of a defunct freezing works. They change quickly, black tactical gear, no patches or colours. This is about the message, not the branding.

Ghost checks his Glock 19. Seventeen rounds plus one in the chamber. Apex carries a suppressed MP5, because of course he does. Sledge has his signature weapon, a cut-down Remington 870 with a pistol grip. And Jester? Jester, was wearing heavy duty knuckle dusters, like some back street brawler, he also had a compound cross bow, strapped to his back and a quiver filled with arrows with a Beretta 92FS side arm on his belt. "Remember," Ghost says, pulling on his balaclava. "We're here for the Serpents. Any civilians, they get a pass."

"There won't be civilians," Apex states. "I pulled the work roster. Night shift is all Serpent-affiliated."

"How do you know that?"

Apex just stares at him. Right. Apex knows everything. It's what makes him valuable. And terrifying.

They move through the industrial park like smoke, using shadows and blind spots that Apex mapped two days ago. The man is nothing if not thorough. They reach the fence line of The Warehouse depot.

"Two guards at the main gate," Sledge whispers. "There's three more men patrolling the grounds. Security cameras on rotating sweeps."

"I've got the cameras," Apex says, pulling out a signal jammer. "Thirty-second window once I activate this."

"Jester, you take the patrol guards," Ghost orders. "Quiet as you can."

"Define quiet."

"No screaming."

"*Their* screaming or mine?"

"*Both.*"

Jester grins beneath his mask. "Where's the fun in that?"

Apex activates the jammer. The security lights flicker momentarily, just enough. Jester vanishes into the dark like he was never there. The man is chaos incarnate, but he moves with unsettling grace when it matters.

Thirty seconds later, three soft thuds echo across the lot. Jester reappears, wiping blood from his rusty knuckle dusters. He gives a thumbs up.

"Show-off," Sledge mutters, but there's affection in it.

They breach the fence where Apex cuts a man-sized hole in exactly twelve seconds. Inside, the depot looms like a sleeping giant. Loading docks line the western wall, and beyond them, the main warehouse where the Crimson Serpents conduct their *real* business, skimming inventory, running protection schemes, planning their expansion into Iron Tide territory.

Ghost signals: Two groups. He and Jester will sweep the loading docks. Sledge and Apex take the main office complex.

They split.

Ghost and Jester move through the loading area, past pallets of flat-screen TVs and kitchen appliances. The smell of cardboard and diesel fuel hangs heavy. Voices echo from deeper in the warehouse.

"...Uncle Dread's finished. The old man's lost his edge..."

"...Iron Tide thinks they own the whole country..."

"...after we take Christchurch, we move on to Greymouth. Cut off their mining contracts..."

Ghost and Jester exchange looks. So this is bigger than a simple territory dispute. The Serpents are planning a full-scale war.

They round a corner, they find them. Eight Crimson Serpents in their red and gold colours, playing cards around a folding table. Weapons within easy reach. Shotguns, pistols, a couple of AR-15s.

Jester whispers, "I've got a joke for you. What's red and gold and black and blue?"

"Don't..."

But Jester's already moving. He vaults over a pallet of microwaves, pulling his fists like loaded firearms from his jacket pockets, and lands in the middle of the card game like an angel of death wearing a half 'n' half mask, representing Jacklyn's sweet smiley face on one side and Hyde's grim brooding face with a mischievous smirk on the other.

"SURPRISE, YOU BASTARDS!..."

Ghost has no choice but to follow. He drops two Serpents with headshots before they can even stand. Jester's brass knuckles become a whirlwind, not elegant, not clean, but devastatingly effective. Blood sprays across pristine retail packaging.

A Serpent gets a shotgun up, but Ghost shoots him through the wrist. The gun clatters away. The man screams. Ghost silences him with a second shot.

Sixty seconds. That's how long it takes. Eight Crimson Serpents, dead or dying, Ghost's heart hasn't even elevated past 90 BPM. Afghanistan taught him that violence, real violence, is just another job.

Jester wipes his mitts on a dead man's jacket. "See? Quiet."

"Your definition of quiet needs work."

Gunfire erupts from the office complex. Sledge and Apex.

They sprint toward the sound, boots pounding concrete. The office complex is a modular structure attached to the warehouse, with cheap walls, cheaper furniture. The door hangs open, riddled with bullet holes.

Inside, they find a massacre.

Apex stands in the center of the main office, MP5 smoking, surrounded by bodies. His tactical gear is immaculate. Not a drop of blood on him. Ten Crimson Serpents lay dead, each with precise double-taps to their bodies core.

But Sledge...

Sledge is across the room, his shotgun forgotten on the floor. He kneels over a body, his hands shaking. The dead man wears Serpent colours, but his face is young. Too young.

"Marcus?" Ghost approaches carefully.

"He's just a kid." Sledge's voice breaks. "Can't be more than twenty."

"He's Serpent affiliated," Apex states coldly. "He made his choice."

"He's somebody's son!" Sledge roars, rounding on Apex. "Somebody's nephew! Just like..."

He can't finish. The weight of his own nephew's death crushes the words.

Ghost moves between them. "Marcus. Brother. I know. But we have a job."

"Yeah." Sledge stands, wiping his eyes behind his mask. "We always have a job, don't we? Another body. Another message. When does it end, Ghost?"

"When Uncle says it ends."

Sledge retrieves his shotgun, not looking at any of them. "Let's finish this."

They find the last targets in a second-floor office, three Serpent commanders huddled around a desk covered in maps and financial documents. These aren't street soldiers. These are the planners. The architects of war.

When the door crashes open, they reach for weapons. Apex cuts them down with surgical precision. The battle is over in seconds.

Ghost approaches the desk, studying the maps. Red circles mark every Iron Tide asset in the South Island. Super markets, general convenience stores franchises, forestry operations, dairy farms. The Serpents weren't just encroaching on The Iron Tide's territory, they'd been planning a complete takeover.

"Photograph everything," he tells Jester. "Uncle needs to see this."

While Jester documents the evidence, Ghost notices something else. It's a leather journal, hand-written. He opens it and freezes.

"Oh, hell."

"What?" Sledge asks.

"They've got people in Parliament. Names. Contact information. Payment records."

Apex peers over his shoulder. "That's Minister Henyard's name. He's the Minister of Conservation."

"Yeah, and he's Iron Tide. It has been for fifteen years." Ghost feels cold dread spreading through his chest. "If the Serpents leaked this information..."

"It would bring down the entire organization," Apex finishes. "Every DOC contract. Every government connection. Uncle's whole political network."

"We need to get this to Waiheke Island," Ghost says. "Now."

They're halfway to their bikes when the police sirens start wailing. Someone must have triggered a silent alarm. The Phantoms sprint through the industrial park, and Ghost's mind races. This was supposed to be a message. Get in, eliminate the threat, get out. But now they're carrying intelligence that could destroy the Iron Tide if it falls into the wrong hands.

They reach their bikes as the first police car skids into the far entrance. Blue and red lights strobe through the darkness.

"MOVE!" Ghost roars.

Four engines scream to life simultaneously. The Phantoms blast out of the industrial park, leaving rubber and noise behind them. Ghost risks a glance in his mirror, three police cars in pursuit, more joining by the second.

State Highway 1 opens up before them. At these speeds, in the dark, one mistake means death. The road becomes a black ribbon of potential catastrophe.

"Split up!" Ghost orders. "Confuse them! Regroup at the safehouse in Greymouth!"

"What about the journal?" Sledge shouts over the comms.

"I've got it!"

They separate at the first intersection. Jester and Apex peel east toward the coast road. Sledge takes a service road south. Ghost continues north, alone, with three police cars locked onto him and a leather journal that contains enough evidence to burn down an empire.

The Suzuki Hayabusa tops 340 kph as Ghost leans into a curve, the centerline becoming a white blur. Behind him, the police cars fall back, they can't match his speed. Ahead, he can see roadblock lights being set up.

They're herding him. Trying to box him in.

Ghost makes a split-second decision. Tapping the brakes a little,changing down a gear. He cuts hard left onto a rural access road at 310 Kph, the bike's tires screaming in protest. Farmland opens up on either side, dark fields and distant mountains. No streetlights. Just the Hayabusa's headlight cutting through absolute darkness.

His heart rate finally elevates. This is where it gets interesting.

The access road becomes gravel, then dirt. Ghost slows down, but not by much. Can't risk slowing down. The journal in his jacket feels like it weighs a thousand kilograms.

He's so focused on the road ahead that he almost misses the spike strip.

Almost.

At the last possible second, Ghost stands on the bike's pegs and yanks the handlebars up, pulling the front wheel skyward. The Hayabusa's back tire hits the spike strip at 200 kph, shredding instantly, and suddenly Ghost is riding a missile with no guidance system.

The bike goes sideways. Ghost separates from it, hitting the dirt road hard enough to see stars. His tactical gear saves his life, The interwoven kevlar padding absorbing impact that would have pulverized bone. He tumbles through the dark, the world spinning, his body ragdoll loose.

When he finally stops rolling, Ghost lies in a field twenty meters from the road, staring up at the Milky Way stretched across the Canterbury sky. His ribs scream. His left shoulder might be dislocated. But he's alive.

And he still has the journal.

Police lights converge on the crash site. Ghost forces himself to his feet, agony lancing through his chest. He stumbles deeper into the field, toward a line of pine trees in the distance. Behind him, he can hear police radios and shouted commands.

"We've got the bike! Spread out! He can't have gone far!"

Ghost reaches the tree line and keeps moving, one agonizing step at a time. The pines give way to native bush, rimu, kahikatea and ferns as tall as a man. New Zealand's ancient forest, dark and alive with sounds. Morepork owls call out their names. Something rustles in the undergrowth, probably a kiwi, maybe a possum or hedge hog.

He pulls out his phone. No signal. Of course not. He's in the middle of nowhere, hunted by police, carrying evidence that could destroy everything Uncle Dread has built.

Ghost finds a hollow beneath a fallen log and crawls inside. The journal presses against his chest. He opens it with trembling hands, using his phone's flashlight to read.

Page after page of names. Government officials. Police commanders. Judges. All on the Iron Tide's payroll. But there are other names too, Crimson Serpent contacts in Tonga, Vanuatu and Australia. The Serpents aren't just local gangs trying to expand. They're part of something bigger. International.

The last page makes Ghost's blood run cold.

A meeting. Scheduled for three days from now. Waiheke Island. Between the Crimson Serpents and someone listed only as "The Architect."

Someone inside the Iron Tide is betraying Uncle Dread.

Ghost closes the journal, his mind reeling. He needs to get this information to Waiheke Island before that meeting happens. But first, he needs to survive the night.

He pulls out his phone again, praying for a signal. One bar. It's enough.

He texts a single number, not Apex or Jester or even Sledge. This goes directly to Uncle Dread on the Chatham Islands.

Found something. BIG. Need extraction. Canterbury bush, 40km south of Christchurch. Compromised.

The reply comes three minutes later.

Help incoming. Stay alive, Ghost. Whatever you have found, keep it safe. The Tide depends on it.

Ghost powers down his phone to save battery and settles in to wait. Around him, the New Zealand bush breathes with nocturnal life. Police sirens wail in the distance. His body aches. His bike is destroyed. And somewhere out there, a traitor is planning to burn down the Iron Tide from the inside.

It's going to be a long night.

CHAPTER TWO: THE FAMILY MAN

T *welve hours earlier - Christchurch suburbs*
Marcus "Sledge" Rawiri stands in his kitchen, making school lunches for his three kids while his wife Sara sleeps upstairs. It's 5:30 AM, and this is his ritual, the moment when he's just Marcus, not Sledge, not a Phantom, not an enforcer for the most powerful criminal organization in New Zealand.

The radio on the shelf above the bench, humming Halsey, "Without Me" and Alex Warren's song, Ordinary. While the humble version of Marcus spread peanut butter and jam sandwiches for Aroha, his seven-year-old. Ham and cheese for Tama, the ten-year-old who's already showing his father's build. And vegetarian everything for Kaia, his thirteen-year-old daughter who decided last month that eating meat was "morally unconscionable."

Marcus smiles despite himself. Where did she even learn that phrase?

His phone buzzes. A text from Ghost: **Wheels up in two hours. Uncle's sending us south.**

The smile fades. Marcus texts back: **Acknowledge. Will be there.**

He finishes the lunches, packs them in the kids' school bags lined up by the door, and goes upstairs. Sara is awake now, sitting up in bed, and the look on her face says she already knows.

"How long?" she asks.

"A few days. Maybe a week."

"Marcus..." Sara's voice cracks. "When does this end? When do you get out?"

It's a conversation they've had a hundred times. Always the same answer. "You know I can't. The Tide doesn't let you walk away."

"Your nephew was *nineteen*, Marcus. Nineteen. And they killed him because he was delivering *money*. When do we admit that our kids could be next?"

Marcus sits on the edge of the bed, takes her hand. "That's exactly why I have to go. The Serpents crossed a line. If we don't respond, we look weak. And weakness gets you dead in this business."

"So instead you go out and make someone else's family grieve?" Sara pulls her hand away. "I married you because you were good. Because you protected people. When did you become the thing you used to fight against?"

The words hit harder than any punch Marcus has ever taken. Because she's right. Ten years ago, he was a bouncer at a Christchurch nightclub, breaking up fights, walking drunk girls to their cars so they'd get home safe. He was a protector.

Then the Iron Tide noticed him. Made him an offer, protection money for the club, and all he had to do was look the other way when their guys conducted business. Easy money. Safe money.

Except there's no such thing as safe money in this life.

One job became two. Two became twenty. Before he knew it, Marcus "Sledge" Rawiri was a Phantom, Uncle Dread's personal enforcer, and there was no going back.

"I'm keeping our kids safe," he says quietly. "Everything I do is to keep them safe."

"By teaching them that violence is how you solve problems? By showing them that loyalty to a gang is more important than loyalty to family?"

"That's not fair..."

"Isn't it?" Sara's eyes are red now, tears threatening. "Aroha drew a picture at school last week. Want to know what it was? Her daddy on a motorcycle with a gun. The teacher called me in for a meeting, Marcus. She's worried about our daughter's 'exposure to violence.'"

Marcus feels something crack inside his chest. He thinks about Uncle Dread's order. The Crimson Serpents. The message they have to send. And he thinks about his nephew's body in the morgue, nineteen years old, his whole life stolen because he was born into the wrong family.

"I have to go," he says, standing. "But when I get back, we'll talk. Really talk. About the future. About getting out."

"You've been saying that for three years."

"I mean it this time."

Sara looks at him with such sadness that Marcus has to turn away. "I hope you do. Because I can't raise our kids in this life anymore. So either you find a way out, or we will."

The ultimatum hangs in the air like smoke.

Marcus showers, changes into his riding gear, and goes to wake the kids. Aroha grumbles about early morning. Tama asks if he can ride his bicycle to school "no" his father says firmly. Kaia barely looks up from her phone, already lost in whatever teenage drama consumes her world.

He kisses each of them goodbye, and none of them know if it might be for the last time.

Present time - _Greymouth safehouse_

The safehouse is a weatherboard cottage on the outskirts of Greymouth, tucked against the bush line where the West Coast rainforest meets civilization. Apex secured it two years ago through a dummy corporation, Iron Tide has dozens of these locations scattered across both islands.

Sledge arrives first, his Kawasaki ZX-14R cutting through the pre-dawn darkness. He kills the engine and sits for a moment, letting the silence settle. His hands shake. They haven't stopped shaking since he saw that kid's body in the Warehouse office.

He was twenty years old. Maybe less. Dead because the Crimson Serpents put him in harm's way.

Just like the Iron Tide puts Sledge in harm's way. Just like Sledge's nephew was put in harm's way.

The cycle never stops. Blood begets blood. Violence begets violence. And somehow, men like Marcus "Sledge" Rawiri tell themselves they're different. They're protecting people. They're providing for their families.

But Sara's right. He's become the thing he used to fight against.

Jester arrives next, his neon-green Kawasaki announcing his presence from a kilometer away. He parks, pulls off his helmet, and grins that mad grin of his.

"Hell of a night! Did you see that one Serpent's face when I..."

"Not now."

Something in Sledge's voice makes Jester's smile falter. "You good, brother?"

"Am I good? We just killed eighteen people, Tommy. *Eighteen*. And for what? Territory? Respect? Because some old man on an island three thousand kilometers away told us to?"

"They killed your nephew, Marcus."

"Yeah. And now we killed somebody else's nephew. Someone else's son. Someone else's brother. When does it end?"

Jester sits down on the cottage steps, uncharacteristically serious. "Are you thinking about getting out?"

"Sara gave me an ultimatum. The Tide, or them."

"Shit, brother. That's heavy."

"What would you do?"

Jester is quiet for a long time. Then: "Honestly? I don't know if guys like us *can* get out. The Tide, the Serpents, the Scorpions, whoever, they don't give exit interviews. You walk away, you're either a threat or a liability. Either way, you end up dead."

"So what, we just keep doing this until someone puts a bullet in us?"

"Or until we're like Uncle Dread, sitting on an island somewhere, pulling strings and living large." Jester laughs, but it sounds hollow.

"Look, I'm not good at the heavy emotional stuff. That's your department. I'm just a funny guy. The chaos merchant. I don't think about the bodies because if I did, I'd probably eat a bullet myself."

Sledge looks at him..., really looks. Behind the jokes and the manic energy, there's something broken in Tommy Finch. Something that's been broken for a very long time.

"We're all broken, aren't we?" Sledge says softly.

"Brother, we were broken before the Tide found us. At least now we're broken together."

They sit in silence as the sun rises, Jester smokes most of his pack of Rothman-Reds . Whilst he scrolled through his phone's new notifications, checked emails and downloaded audio media. Starlip satellites providing perfect rural internet as his downloads, pumped out cutting the what would have been deathly silence mixed with tension.

Not that Jesters jukebox mixed selection chilled the nerves, much. Bands such as "MegaDeath" and their "Symphony of Destruction", "System of Down", "Ariels", "Papa Roach" and the "Last Resort". Artists like NF and his rap, "When I Grow Up". Kendrick Lemar, "Not Like Us". "Eminem and his lyrical"Venom '","Knock-Knock"and "Monster", mixes. Topping them all off with Marlyn Manson's "Beautiful People".

The night's darkness gives way as the sun starts to rise over the Tasman Sea, painting the sky in golds and pinks. It should be beautiful. But all Sledge can see is blood.

Apex arrives at 7 AM, his Ducati purring to a stop with mechanical precision. He dismounts, runs a quick diagnostic check on the bike (because of course he does), and only then acknowledges the others.

"No word from Ghost," he states. "His phone's been dark for six hours."

"He'll make contact when he can," Jester says. "Ghost is unkillable. Like a cockroach, but cooler."

"He crashed doing 200 kph," Apex counters. "Hit a spike strip. Even if he survived, he's injured and on foot in hostile territory with every cop in Canterbury looking for him."

"So what do we do?" Sledge asks.

"We wait for orders from Uncle Dread. If Ghost found something important enough to risk that run, it'll be worth it."

"And if he's dead?"

Apex meets Sledge's eyes, and there's something frightening in his gaze. "Then we avenge him. Like we always do."

Sledge's phone rings. Unknown number. He answers: "Yeah?"

"Marcus Rawiri?" A woman's voice, professional, cold.

"Who's asking?"

"My name is Detective Senior Sergeant Kate Morrison, New Zealand Police. We need to talk about your nephew, Tyler."

Sledge's blood runs cold. "I already talked to you people. I don't know who killed him."

"Actually, I think you do. I think you know exactly who killed him, and I think you're currently in Greymouth preparing to retaliate. Am I wrong?"

Silence.

"Mr. Rawiri, I've been investigating the Iron Tide for four years. I know what you are. I know what you do. And I'm calling to tell you that if you continue down this path, you're going to destroy yourself and your family."

"Are you threatening me?"

"I'm offering you a way out. We can protect you. Your wife, your kids. Witness protection, new identities, new lives. All you have to do is cooperate."

Sledge laughs bitterly. "You don't know Uncle Dread. There's nowhere you can hide me that the Tide won't eventually find. And when they do..."

"When they do, you'll be dead. Just like your nephew. Is that what you want for Aroha? For Tama? For Kaia? You want them to grow up without a father? Or worse..., you want them to follow your path, in your personal foot steps or boot prints, tire tracks perhaps for what of a better expression or perhaps ending your...soul trading..., moonlit career?"

"How do you know my kids' names?"

"Because I've done my homework, Marcus. I know everything about you. Where you live. What school your kids attend. Where your wife works. I know you coach Kaia's netball team. I know Tama wants to be a marine biologist. I know Aroha still sleeps with a nightlight because she's afraid of the dark."

Rage floods through Sledge. "If you touch, or so much, go near my family..."

Kate interrupts abruptly. "I am not threatening them. I'm trying to save them. From you. From the life you've chosen. From the violence that's coming next."

"What do you mean, 'violence that's coming'?"

Detective Morrison's voice drops. "The Crimson Serpents aren't your only problem. There's someone inside the Iron Tide feeding information to law enforcement. We call him Oracle. He's been giving us everything, operations, safe houses, financial records. The entire organization is about to come crashing down, and when it does, anyone still inside will go down with it."

"You're lying."

"Am I? Then explain how we knew about the Warehouse hit last night before you even arrived. Explain how we knew exactly which route Ghost would take, exactly where to set up the spike strip. Oracle told us everything."

The words hit Sledge like a jackhammer. Someone inside the Iron Tide is a traitor. Someone they trust.

"I don't believe you."

"Then don't believe me. But when Uncle Dread's empire burns, and you're standing next to the royal throne surrounded by ashes wondering how it all went wrong, remember this conversation. Remember that I offered you a way out, and you chose the Tide."

The line goes dead.

Sledge stands there, phone in hand, his mind racing. A traitor. Oracle. Someone feeding information to the police.

He looks at Apex and Jester, studying their faces. Could it be one of them? Could it be Ghost?

Could it be him?

"Who was that?" Apex asks.

"Wrong number," Sledge lies.

But the seed has been planted. Doubt. Suspicion. The most corrosive thing in any criminal organization.

The Iron Tide is about to tear itself apart from the inside.

CHAPTER THREE: THE ARCHITECT

Waiheke Island - <u>Three days before the meeting</u>

Uncle Dread's compound sits on the eastern edge of Waiheke Island, disguised as a luxury vineyard estate. Tourists sipping Sauvignon Blanc at the cellar door have no idea that beneath the barrel room, a command center coordinates an empire worth billions.

Richard "The Baron" Branston pours himself a whiskey and watches the Auckland skyline glitter across the Hauraki Gulf. At sixty-seven, Branston looks like a kind grandfather, silver beard, warm smile, the kind of man who'd give you directions and mean it.

He's also the Iron Tide's primary financier and one of the most ruthless men in the Southern Hemisphere.

"Tell me about the journal," Uncle Dread says, his voice carrying across the underground facility.

The Baron swirls his drink. "Ghost found their entire operational blueprint. Names, dates, financial transfers. But more importantly, he found evidence of the Oracle."

"This traitor."

"Yes. Someone in your inner circle has been feeding information to both the Serpents and the police. Someone with access to everything."

Uncle Dread's face remains impassive, but his hands grip the armrests of his chair. "The Phantoms?"

"Possibly. Or someone in the Council."

The Council. Seven men and women who manage the Iron Tide's various operations. Each one vetted, loyal, essential. The idea that one of them could be Oracle makes Uncle Dread's blood run cold.

"I want them all here," he says quietly. "For the meeting. Every Council member. Every Phantom. Everyone who knows the full extent of our operations."

"That's dangerous. Putting everyone in one place."

"It's necessary. Oracle will reveal themselves. They won't be able to resist the opportunity."

The Baron nods slowly. "And when they do?"

Uncle Dread's smile is colder than the Antarctic wind. "Then we'll remind them why betraying the Iron Tide is always fatal."

Meanwhile in: Mount Eden Prison, Auckland

Victor "Apex" Drummond walks through the prison corridors like he owns them. In a sense, he does. Half the guards are on the Iron Tide payroll. The other half are too scared to interfere.

He's not here as an inmate. He's here for a meeting.

Cell Block D, maximum security. This is where the Iron Tide keeps its most valuable asset: Thomas "Prophet" Keane, a former chartered accountant who'd been caught embezzling from his firm. The Iron Tide offered him a choice, twenty years in prison, or work for them from the inside.

The Prophet chose survival.

Now he runs the prison's cryptocurrency operation, laundering millions through digital wallets that exist only in the blockchain's shadow. Bitcoin, Ethereum, Monero, all flowing through Prophet's fingers, cleaned and distributed to Iron Tide shell companies across the Pacific.

"Apex." The Prophet looks up from his laptop, a device that shouldn't exist in maximum security but somehow does. "I heard about Christchurch. Eighteen bodies."

"Seventeen. One survived."

"That's not like Ghost to leave loose ends."

Apex sits across from the Prophet, his eyes flat and dangerous. "Ghost is compromised. Missing for twelve hours. I need to know if anyone's been accessing our offshore accounts."

The Prophet's fingers dance across the keyboard. Numbers cascade down the screen in green phosphorescent waterfalls. "Define 'anyone.'"

"Someone with Council-level access. Someone who might be liquidating assets."

The room falls silent except for the clicking of keys. Then the Prophet freezes.

"Oh, shit."

"What?"

"Someone's been siphoning funds. Small amounts, spread across dozens of transactions. I almost missed it because they're using legitimate operational codes." Prophet looks up, his face pale. "Whoever this is, they're good. Really good. And they've been doing it for eighteen months."

"How much?"

"Forty-two million. Maybe more."

Apex's jaw tightens. Forty-two million dollars, stolen from under Uncle Dread's nose. Oracle isn't just feeding information to enemies, they're robbing the organization blind.

"Can you trace it?"

"I can try, but they're using mixers and tumblers. It'll take time."

"You have seventy-two hours. Before the Waiheke meeting."

The Prophet nods grimly. "If I find them?"

"You tell me. Only me. Not Uncle Dread. Not Ghost. Just me."

Something flickers across the Prophet's face. Suspicion? Fear? "Why the secrecy?"

Apex leans forward. "Because if Oracle is one of the Phantoms, I need to know before they reach Waiheke. Otherwise, Uncle Dread might be walking into an execution."

Canterbury bush: Dawn

Ghost wakes to the sound of a helicopter.

His entire body screams in protest as he crawls out of his hiding spot beneath the fallen log. Through the canopy, he can see the chopper circling, it is black in colour, unmarked, definitely not police.

His phone buzzes. A text from an unknown number: *Extraction in five. Clear the LZ.*

Ghost stumbles into a small clearing, every step agony. His left shoulder is definitely dislocated. At least two ribs are cracked. But he's alive, and he still has the journal.

The helicopter descends, rotors thrashing the ferns into a frenzy. The side door opens, and Ghost sees a face he wasn't expecting.

Marcus "Sledge" Rawiri.

"Need a lift?" Sledge shouts over the rotor wash.

Ghost half-runs, half-collapses toward the helicopter. Sledge hauls him inside with surprising gentleness. As they lift off, Ghost sees police cars converging on the clearing below, too late by seconds.

"How did you find me?" Ghost gasps.

"Apex triangulated your last known position. Jester hacked the police dispatch to track their search patterns. And Uncle Dread called in a favour with a guy who owns a helicopter tour company."

Ghost manages a weak laugh. "The Baron?"

"Who else?"

The helicopter banks north, following the coastline toward Greymouth. Ghost clutches the journal to his chest, feeling its weight, its terrible importance.

"Marcus. There's something you need to know."

"About Oracle?"

Ghost's eyes snap to Sledge's face. "You know about Oracle?"

"Detective Morrison called me. Tried to flip me. Said Oracle's been feeding information to the cops for months."

"It's worse than that." Ghost opens the journal to the last page, showing Sledge the entry about the Waiheke meeting. "Oracle's been working with the Crimson Serpents. This whole war? It's a setup. They wanted us to retaliate, wanted us to expose our operations and wanted us to be angry and reckless."

"Why?"

"Because someone wants to take over the Iron Tide. Someone who knows how Uncle Dread thinks, how we operate, where our vulnerabilities are."

Sledge's face goes gray. "Someone on the Council."

"Or one of us."

The two Phantoms stare at each other. Years of brotherhood, of bleeding together, of trusting each other with their lives. And now?

Now everything is suspect.

"I need to ask you something," Ghost says carefully. "Where were you when my bike got spiked?"

"Are you seriously asking me if I'm Oracle?"

"I'm asking where you were."

Sledge's fists clench. "I was riding to Greymouth. Alone. Which means I could've made a phone call. Set up the spike strip. Is that what you want to hear?"

"Marcus..."

"No. You want to know if I betrayed you? If I'm the one who killed your nephew, my nephew? If I'm the reason eighteen bodies are cooling in a Christchurch warehouse?"

"Someone had to tell the cops where we'd be."

"Yeah. Someone did." Sledge leans close, his voice dropping to something dangerous. "But it wasn't me. So either you trust me, Ghost, or you put a bullet in me right now. Because I'm not spending the next three days wondering if my best friend thinks I'm a traitor."

The helicopter shudders through turbulence. Ghost studies Sledge's face, looking for deception, for guilt, for anything that might reveal the truth.

He finds only pain.

"I trust you," Ghost finally says.

"Do you?"

"I have to. Because if I can't trust you, I can't trust anyone. And if I can't trust anyone..." He doesn't finish the thought.

Sledge nods slowly. "The meeting on Waiheke. Three days from now. That's when Oracle will make their move."

"That's when we'll be ready."

K' Road: <u>Auckland's underbelly</u>

Karangahape Road at midnight is a neon fever dream, strip clubs, tattoo parlors, late-night kebab shops. The kind of bars where asking the wrong question gets your teeth kicked in!

Tommy "Jester" Finch loves it here.

He parks his Kawasaki outside The Purple Serpent, a club owned by Crown Entertainment, one of the Iron Tide's many fronts. Inside, the bass pounds hard enough to feel in your chest. Bodies writhe on the dance floor under UV lights.The clubs Walls reverberating Cardi B's "Wap","Bodiaks Yellow". "The Weekends", "Earned It" and "G Easy's", "I mean It".

Jester isn't here for pleasure. He's here for intelligence.

Stephen "The King" Crowley holds court in the VIP section, surrounded by women half his age and men who'd kill for him without question. At seventy-one, Crowley is a legendary pornographer, promoter, provocateur. His "Bits on Bikes" parade scandalized Auckland society for years. Now he launders Iron Tide money through his network of adult entertainment venues.

"Jester!" Crowley waves him over, grinning. "Heard your boys made a mess down south!"

"You know me. Go big or go home."

Crowley laughs, but his eyes are calculating. "Uncle Dread's calling everyone to Waiheke. Big meeting. You know what it's about?"

"Spring cleaning?"

"Don't be cute. Word is there's a traitor. Someone is selling us out." Crowley leans close, whiskey-breath hot against Jester's ear. "Between you and me? I think it's one of the Council. Someone got greedy."

"Got any names?"

"If I did, they'd already be dead." Crowley sits back, watching Jester carefully. "You Phantoms, you're Uncle Dread's golden boys. But even gold tarnishes eventually. Just make sure you're on the right side when the hammer falls."

Jester forces a laugh, playing the fool he's famous for being. But inside, his mind races. Crowley knows something. And whatever it is, it's dangerous enough that even this old wolf is scared.

BLOOD AND BROTHERHOOD

CHAPTER FOUR: THE WAIHEKE RECKONING

The compound on Waiheke Island feels like a mausoleum. Thirty-seven people gather in Uncle Dread's underground command center, each one essential to the Iron Tide's operations, each one now a suspect. The Council members sit in their designated chairs around the obsidian table, seven faces carved from ambition and survival. The Phantoms stand against the back wall, Ghost still favoring his injured shoulder, Sledge's hands trembling slightly, Jester's usual manic energy subdued, Apex watching everything with those dead, calculating eyes.

Uncle Dread enters last, moving with the deliberate slowness of a man who knows he holds absolute power. At eighty-three, he should be fragile. Instead, he radiates menace like heat from a furnace.

"Someone in this room," he begins, his voice soft as falling ash, "is called Oracle."

The silence that follows could suffocate.

"Oracle has stolen forty-two million dollars from our accounts. Oracle has fed information to the Crimson Serpents and the New Zealand Police. Oracle has put every single person in this organization at risk." Uncle Dread's eyes move across the assembled faces like a searchlight. "Oracle thought they were clever. Thought they could take what belongs to the Iron Tide and walk away clean."

Richard "The Baron" Branston stands, activating a screen behind Uncle Dread. Financial transactions cascade down in glowing columns. "These are unauthorized transfers. Small amounts, carefully hidden, routed through cryptocurrency mixers and offshore accounts. Whoever Oracle is, they understand our systems intimately."

"It's one of the Council," someone shouts. Matt Chen, who runs the forestry operations. "It has to be! Only Council members have that level of access!"

"Or one of the Phantoms," counters Helena Bright, who manages the parliamentary connections. Her eyes fix on Ghost. "How convenient that you survived the police ambush. How convenient that you 'found' this journal with all our secrets written down."

Ghost steps forward, rage blazing across his face. "Are you calling me a traitor?"

"I'm saying it's suspicious."

"Suspicious?" Ghost's hand drops to his waist, where his Glock sits in its holster. "I crashed at 200 kph. I spent twelve hours hiding in the bush with broken ribs. I brought you evidence of a massive conspiracy, and you're accusing *me*?"

Apex moves to Ghost's side, his voice cold as a morgue slab. "Helena, if Ghost wanted to betray us, he'd have given that journal to the cops instead of nearly dying to bring it here."

"Unless that's exactly what he wants us to think."

The room erupts. Accusations fly like shrapnel. Council members pointing fingers at each other. Phantoms glaring at Council members. The entire command center devolved into chaos.

And Marcus "Sledge" Rawiri stands frozen, his mind a thousand kilometers away.

Because three hours ago, he received a text message. From Sara. His wife. The mother of his children.

I'm sorry. I had to protect them. Detective Morrison promised us safety. Please understand. I love you.

Sledge had stared at those words until they blurred. Sara. His Sara. The woman who'd begged him to leave the Iron Tide. The woman who'd given him an ultimatum.

She'd been feeding information to Detective Morrison all along.

But that wasn't the worst part. The worst part was the second message, from an unknown number.

Your wife isn't Oracle. But she's been useful. Tell anyone, and Aroha, Tama, and Kaia disappear. You have until the Waiheke meeting to decide whose side you're on.

Sledge's children. Hostages. Leverage. His family being used as weapons against him.

He looks around the room at his brothers, his comrades, the people he's bled beside for six years. Ghost, who saved his life in a Dunedin shootout. Apex, who helped him move into his first house. Jester, who bought birthday presents for his kids every year without being asked.

And then he thinks about Aroha's laugh. Tama's dreams of becoming a marine biologist. Kaia's fierce idealism.

What is loyalty worth when measured against your children's lives?

"ENOUGH!" Uncle Dread's voice cracks like a whip. The room falls silent. "We will not tear ourselves apart. That's exactly what Oracle wants. So here's what's going to happen."

He gestures to The Baron, who produces a metal briefcase. Inside, five keys, each attached to a different coloured fob.

"Tomorrow night," Uncle Dread continues, "the Crimson Serpents are planning their final assault. They think we're weak, divided, vulnerable. They're going to hit every Iron Tide asset simultaneously, supermarkets, forestry camps, our parliamentary contacts, everything. One coordinated strike designed to destroy us completely."

"How do you know this?" Ghost asks.

"Because Oracle told them when to attack. Oracle gave them our entire defensive network. Oracle thinks they've set us up for slaughter." Uncle Dread's smile is terrifying. "But Oracle made one critical mistake. They forgot who they're dealing with."

He opens another case. Inside, maps marked with red circles. Dozens of them. Hundreds.

"These are Crimson Serpent locations across the North Island. Clubhouses, meth labs, weapons caches, leadership homes. Every single one." Uncle Dread's eyes gleam. "While they're attacking us, we're going to erase them from existence."

"That's suicide," Helena Bright says. "We don't have the numbers for a full-scale war."

"We don't need numbers." Uncle Dread holds up the keys. "We have something better. We have the Arsenal."

CHAPTER FIVE: THE ARSENAL

The Fort Knox safehouse sits at Cape Reinga, New Zealand's northernmost point, where the Tasman Sea and Pacific Ocean collide in a perpetual battle of currents. Māori legend says this is where spirits leap into the underworld.

Tonight, it's where legends are born.

The Phantoms arrive at Cape Reinga right at midnight, escorted by Uncle Dread himself. The safehouse looks like an ordinary old light house station. The viewing platform sits on a popular tourist attraction by day. It doesn't appear out of the ordinary in any way.

Some of them have stood there many times before and taken their pictures next to the global direction sign post marker. The outside is mostly constructed of concrete and brick,with an ancient weathered ladder dangling from its side, its rungs just out of reach.

The whole exterior of the building was painted with layer upon layer of peeling pale white paint, faded solar panels on the roof. Nothing to suggest it's one of the most secure facilities in the Southern Hemisphere lies beneath it...

Uncle Dread places his palm against a scanner hidden in the doorframe. Retinal scan. Voice recognition. DNA verification. The door unlocks with a hiss of pressurized air.

Inside, the building is deceptive. The main room looks lived-in, cluttered with ranger gear and topographical maps. But Uncle Dread presses a section of wall, the floor jars 'n' ripples then starts descending like an elevator,sliding down an ancient mining shaft. The moving platform creeps onward, descending into darkness.

"How deep does this go?" Jester whispers.Nervously, but deep down he's highly pressurised with anticipation almost to the point of internally, spontaneously combusting into flames. Like some kind of menacing Phoenix.

"Forty meters," Apex answers. Because of course he already knows.

They descend in silence now, well for the most part. Marcus can't get a song out his head, so now he's whistling the tune aloud. George Thorogood and the Destroyer's, antagonistic lyrics "Bad to the Bone" the lipped pitches echoing off concrete walls. Motion sensors track their progress. Gun turrets, thankfully inactive, bristle from the ceiling. This isn't just a safehouse. It's a fortress.

The staircase opens into a vast underground chamber carved from living rock. Industrial lighting flickers to life, row after row of fluorescent tubes illuminating what can only be described as a cathedral of speed.

"Holy shit," Ghost breathes. Marcus splutters and coughs clearing his throat, and stammers the words, Woooow... this place really is bad to the bone, he barely spits the words out. His mind now racing in pure amazement. How could something like this remain a secret?

In front of them were motorcycles. Dozens of them. But they were not any ordinary bikes. These are fever dreams made metal, engineering pushed past sanity into the realm of pure, beautiful madness.

Uncle Dread walks to the center of the chamber, his footsteps echoing. "The Arsenal !". Forty years of preparation. Every bike you see here represents a project I commissioned, funded, or stole. Some are prototypes. Some are one-of-ones. All of them are illegal for road use. All of them are faster than anything the Serpents or N.Z police can throw at us."

He gestures grandly. "Choose your weapons, Phantoms. Tonight, you ride into legend."

The first bike stops Sledge in his tracks. It shouldn't exist. Can't exist. But there it is, chrome and carbon fiber gleaming under harsh lights.

A John Britten V1000. New Zealand's most legendary motorcycle, designed and hand-built by John Britten in the 1990s. Only ten were ever made. This one... this one is different.

"Is that..." Sledge can't finish the sentence.

"A Britten?" Uncle Dread nods. "Not quite. This is what Britten was building when he died. The V1200. Bigger engine, forced induction, computer-controlled everything. I bought the plans from his widow, hired his original team, and finished what he started."

Uncle Dread runs his hand along the bike's sculpted bodywork with something approaching reverence. "Supercharged V-twin, 1,200cc. Somewhere north of 280 horsepower. Titanium frame. Carbon fibered everything else. It weighs less than your daughter, Marcus, and makes more power than a small car. It'll do 380 kilometers per hour if you're brave enough."

Sledge stares at the machine. It's art. It's violence. It's everything the Iron Tide represents distilled into two wheels and an engine.

"That's yours," Uncle Dread says quietly. "If you want it."

Next to the Britten sits Uncle Dread's personal mount. The Vincent Black Shadow from the old photographs, but transformed. The original engine has been bored out, fitted with a turbocharger the size of a basketball. Intercoolers snake around the frame. Custom ECU. Nitrous injection. The entire bike radiates barely-contained fury.

"1,000cc V-twin producing 240 horsepower," Uncle Dread says proudly. "It'll rip your arms off if you're not careful. I've been saving this ride for something special. Tomorrow qualifies."

Ghost gravitates toward a Suzuki Hayabusa that looks like it ate another Hayabusa and absorbed its power. Twin turbochargers protrude from the bodywork like weapons. The fuel tank has been replaced with a cell that probably holds race gas or worse.

"Unlimited class drag bike," Uncle Dread explains. "380 horsepower. Quarter-mile in 7.2 seconds at 320 kph. Completely unstable, utterly ridiculous, and faster than God. Sound familiar, Ghost?"

Ghost grins despite himself. "It's perfect."

Apex doesn't hesitate. He walks straight to a matte-black Kawasaki H2R that's been further modified into something that looks actively hostile. The factory supercharger has been upgraded. The exhaust system is pure race-spec. NASA-grade materials, Uncle Dread said, and looking at this machine, it's believable.

"340 horsepower," Apex says, reading the specs printed on a placard. "Launch control, traction control, probably has an AI that makes tactical decisions." He looks at Uncle Dread. "This is military hardware disguised as a motorcycle."

"Exactly."

Jester practically vibrates with excitement as he approaches a streetfighter-style Suzuki B-King that's been taken to absolutely deranged extremes. Nitrous bottles where the passenger seat should be. Underglow LED lights. A sound system that can probably deafen pedestrians. The paint job is neon chaos, electric blue and acid green and violent pink all fighting for dominance.

"Please tell me this one's mine," Jester begs.

"Turbocharged, 1,400cc, nitrous injection, and a top speed nobody's been stupid enough to test," Uncle Dread confirms. "It's loud, it's obnoxious, and it'll either make you famous or kill you spectacularly. Probably both."

"I'm in love."

But there are other machines here too. A MTT Y2K Turbine Superbike, powered by an actual helicopter engine. A Dodge Tomahawk concept that looks like it escaped from a science fiction film. Multiple Suzukis, an RG570 fully equipped with an aftermarket big bore kit, titanium pistons and forged rings with a full carbon fiber frame that probably weighs less than a bicycle, a GSX1400 built for torque and brutality, a supercharged Yamaha R1 painted in Iron Tide colours.

And in the back, almost hidden, a Honda RC30 that's been upgraded with modern everything while maintaining its classic beauty.

"Gentleman," Uncle Dread says, and his voice carries weight that makes them all turn. "These machines represent forty years of my life. Forty years of building something that matters. Tomorrow night, the Crimson Serpents are going to try to take everything we've built. Everything we've bled for. Everything we are."

He pauses, letting the words sink in.

"But here's what I'm offering you. You ride these bikes into battle tomorrow. You help me destroy the Serpents utterly and completely. And when the smoke clears?" Uncle Dread's smile is fierce. "You each get signed deeds to equal shares of the entire Iron Tide. Not just soldiers. Not just Phantoms. Partners. Owners. Kings."

The silence is absolute.

"You're serious," Ghost says.

"I'm eighty-three years old. I'm tired. And I've realized something." Uncle Dread looks at each of them in turn. "Empires don't die when their founders die. They die when their founders fail to pass the torch to people worthy of carrying it forward. You four? You're worthy. You've proven that a thousand times over."

"What about the Council?" Apex asks.

"Fuck the Council. They're administrators. Accountants. Politicians. You're warriors. You're the ones who bleed. You're the ones who risk everything." Uncle Dread's voice drops to something almost gentle. "You're the sons I never had. And tomorrow, I'm going to fight beside you one last time before I hand you the kingdom."

Sledge feels something crack inside his chest. Sons. Uncle Dread, he actually called them sons.

And all Sledge can think about is Sara's text message. The threat against his children. The impossible choice bearing down on him like a collapsing building.

"What if one of us is Oracle?" The words escape before Sledge can stop them.

Everyone turns to stare.

"What if Oracle is in this room right now?" Sledge continues, his voice gaining strength. "What if everything you just offered us is exactly what Oracle wants? Access to everything. Power. Control. What if this whole meeting is a trap?"

Uncle Dread studies him for a long moment. "Then Oracle is about to learn a valuable lesson."

"Which is?"

"That betraying the Iron Tide is always fatal. Even if you win, you lose." Uncle Dread walks to Sledge, close enough that only the Phantoms can hear his next words. "I know one of you might be Oracle. I've known for weeks. But here's the thing about rats, Marcus. Eventually, they always reveal themselves. And when they do? The trap snaps shut."

He steps back, addressing all of them. "Tomorrow night, we ride. The Serpents die. And Oracle..." Uncle Dread's smile is terrible. "Oracle learns that some empires can't be stolen. Only inherited by those strong enough to hold them."

The Phantoms spend the night in the Arsenal, prepping bikes, checking weapons, and avoiding each other's eyes. The camaraderie is fractured now, poisoned by suspicion and doubt.

Ghost works on his turbo Hayabusa in silence, methodically checking every system. Apex runs diagnostics on the H2R with mechanical precision. Jester tries to maintain his usual energy, cracking jokes that fall flat, his laughter echoing hollow in the underground chamber.

And Sledge? Sledge sits on the Britten V1200, not moving, his mind a warzone. One ear phone plugged in his ear, playing tunes by KAYDUB.

Sara's text message burns in his pocket. His children's faces haunt him. Aroha's laugh. Tama's dreams. Kaia's fierce idealism. Everything he's fought to protect.

But on the other hand: Ghost, who saved his life. Apex, who never abandoned him. Jester, who brought joy to his darkest days. Uncle Dread, who called him son.

How do you choose between family and brotherhood?

How do you choose between blood and loyalty?

How do you choose between love and honor?

"You're thinking too hard." Jester appears beside him, startling Sledge from his thoughts. "I can hear your brain grinding from across the room."

"Just... processing."

"Yeah." Jester sits on his own bike, the modified B-King. "Heavy stuff. End of the world type vibes." He pauses. "You know what the worst part is? I don't even know who I'm supposed to be suspicious of anymore. Is it you? Is it Ghost? Is it me?" He laughs bitterly. "Maybe I'm Oracle and I just don't know it yet. Maybe we're all Oracle. Maybe Oracle is the friends we made along the way."

"Tommy..."

"I'm scared, Marcus." The admission comes quietly. "I'm actually genuinely terrified. Because tomorrow we're going to war, and I don't know if we're fighting for the right side anymore. Hell, I don't even know if there is a right side."

Sledge looks at his friend, really looks at him. Behind the jokes and chaos, Tommy Finch is just a broken kid who found purpose in violence. They all are. Broken kids playing at being warriors, pretending their scars make them strong instead of just damaged.

"I need to tell you something," Sledge says.

"Please don't tell me you're Oracle. I don't think my heart could take it."

"Sara's been feeding information to Detective Morrison."

Jester goes very still. "Your wife?"

"She thought she was protecting our kids. Morrison promised witness protection, new identities, new lives. Sara thought..." Sledge's voice cracks. "She thought she was saving us."

"Oh, brother." Jester's hand finds Sledge's shoulder. "That's heavy. That's really heavy."

"But she's not Oracle. Someone else is using her. Using my family as leverage. I got a message threatening my kids if I don't..." He can't finish.

"If you don't, what?"

"I don't know. That's the problem. I don't know what they want from me. Stay silent? Betray everyone? Run?" Sledge looks at Jester with desperate eyes. "What would you do?"

"Honestly? I'd probably make the wrong choice. I'm really good at that." Jester manages a weak smile. "But here's what I know about you, Marcus Rawiri. You're the most loyal person I've ever met. You love hard, you protect fiercely, and you'd die before you let anyone hurt the people you care about. So whatever you decide? It'll be because you're trying to do right by everyone. And that's all any of us can do."

"What if doing right by everyone is impossible?"

"Then you do right by yourself. You make the choice you can live with. Because after tomorrow?" Jester stands, heading back to his bike. "We might not be alive to regret anything anyway."

Dawn breaks over the lighthouse, like the world catching fire. The Phantoms and Uncle Dread stand outside the safehouse, their bikes lined up like war horses before battle. The modified machines gleam in the early light, beautiful and menacing.

Uncle Dread mounts his turbo Vincent, and for a moment, the years fall away. He's not an eighty-three-year-old crime lord. He's a young rider again, wild and free and unstoppable.

"Gentlemen," he says, his voice carrying over the wind. "Today, the Iron Tide reminds New Zealand who rules these islands. Today, we show the Serpents what happens when you challenge gods. Today..."

He starts the Vincent's engine. It roars like thunder, like violence, like everything primal and savage and free.

"Today, we ride into legend!"

Four more engines scream to life. The Britten V1200. The turbo Hayabusa. The H2R. The mad B-King. Five riders, five machines, each one capable of speeds that defy sanity.

They launch south from Cape Reinga as the sun rises, a formation of mechanical fury racing toward war. The countryside blurs past at impossible velocities. State Highway 1 becomes a ribbon of asphalt designed specifically for this moment, for these riders, for this reckoning.

At 350 kilometers per hour, Sledge feels something like peace.

The Britten V1200 responds to his thoughts before his hands move. The supercharger whines like a living thing. The titanium frame transmits every nuance of the road directly to his body. He is the bike. The bike is him. Man and machine merged into a single entity of purpose and speed.

And in that moment of clarity, Marcus "Sledge" Rawiri makes his choice.

His family. Always his family.

He reaches for his phone, texts a number he memorized but never called.

Detective Morrison. It's Sledge. I'm in. Whatever you need. But my kids stay safe. That's non-negotiable.

The reply comes instantly.

Thank you, Marcus. You're doing the right thing. When the fighting starts tonight, make sure you're nowhere near Uncle Dread. What's coming for him... you don't want to be there.

Sledge deletes the messages and tucks his phone away. Guilt crushes his chest like a physical weight. But his children's faces shine in his mind like salvation.

He's made his choice.

Now he has to live with it.

CHAPTER SIX: THE BLOOD HOUR

Auckland. 8:47 PM.

The Crimson Serpents make their move precisely as Oracle predicted. Coordinated strikes across the entire North Island. Teams hit Iron Tide supermarket protection contracts in Wellington, Palmerston North, Hamilton, Tauranga. Forestry camps in Rotorua burn. Parliamentary offices in the Beehive receive suspicious packages. The assault is surgical, brutal, and perfectly timed.

The Serpents think they're winning.

They have no idea what's coming.

Uncle Dread and the Phantoms split up, each taking different targets. The plan is simple: overwhelming violence delivered with such speed and precision that the Serpents never have time to react.

Ghost hits the Serpent clubhouse in South Auckland. His turbo Hayabusa launches him into the parking lot at 200 kph, sliding sideways in a controlled drift that sends gravel spraying like shrapnel. He's off the bike before it stops moving, Glock 19 in hand, and the night erupts into controlled chaos.

Serpents pour out of the clubhouse, confused, arming themselves, shouting orders. Ghost is already inside. His military training takes over, muscle memory, breathing control, target acquisition. He moves through the building like smoke, like death, like everything the Iron Tide represents.

Fifteen Serpents down in under three minutes. Ghost extracts before the police arrive, the Hayabusa screaming back into the night with its rider painted in other people's blood.

Jester targets a Serpent meth lab in Manukau. His approach is less surgical. He rides the modified B-King straight through the lab's front door, nitrous injection engaged, the bike's engine shrieking like a demon being born.

The explosion that follows is spectacular.

Jester tumbles clear as the building erupts in flames, the meth supplies cooking off like fireworks. He lies on his back in the parking lot, laughing hysterically, covered in ash and glory.

"LIKE AND SUBSCRIBE, MOTHERFUCKERS!" he screams at the burning building.Jester pulls his phone out. The screen is damaged but he is able to scroll his old music list looking for the next song to play. " hmm which one would go well with that helmet cam footage, lets see theres. Classic Rob Zombie, Limpizkit, Linkin Park. Or a more recent file downloaded into his playlist. Kalmi's,Hanumankind-Big Dawgs.

Later, Ghost will yell at him for the unnecessary theatrics. Right now, thirty million dollars worth of Serpent infrastructure is turning into smoke and ruin, and Jester couldn't be happier.

Apex approaches his target with characteristic precision. The Serpent's main weapons cache, hidden in a storage facility in West Auckland. He doesn't announce himself. Doesn't make noise. He simply appears, the H2R parked in shadows, and systematically eliminates every guard.

Suppressed MP5. Headshots. Professional. Clean.

Then he sets charges throughout the facility, high-grade military explosives that definitely shouldn't be in civilian hands. Apex activates the timer, mounts his bike, and is three kilometers away when the storage facility vanishes in a fireball that lights up the Auckland sky.

The blast wave breaks windows for two blocks. The sound echoes off the Waitematoi Harbour like an angry god clearing their throat.

Apex permits himself a small smile. Precision instruments, wielded with precision violence.

Uncle Dread rides toward the center of Auckland, toward the Crimson Serpent's headquarters in the CBD. This is the heart of their operation, where their leadership coordinates the assault on the Iron Tide. This is where the war will be won or lost.

The turbo Vincent screams through city streets at velocities that make pedestrians scatter and cars swerve. Uncle Dread rides like a young man again, fearless, reckless, alive in ways he hasn't felt in decades.

This is what he was born for. This moment. This reckoning.

He bursts into the Serpent headquarters like a comet. The Vincent slid to a stop in the lobby, its turbo spooling down with a sound like a banshee's wail. Serpent soldiers reach for weapons.

Uncle Dread draws faster.

Two shots. Two bodies. Then he's moving, his eighty-three-year-old body moving with the muscle memory of a lifetime's violence. More shots. More bodies. The lobby becomes a slaughterhouse.

He reaches the elevator, rides it to the top floor where the Serpent's council meets. The doors open to reveal ten men in red and gold, armed, waiting.

"Uncle Dread," the head Serpent says. His name is Drake "Komodo" Williams, a Samoan enforcer with a reputation for extreme violence. "You came alone. That's brave. Or stupid."

"I came to deliver a message."

"Which is?"

Uncle Dread smiles, and it's the most terrifying thing any of them have ever seen. "The Iron Tide doesn't forgive. The Iron Tide doesn't forget. And the Iron Tide never loses."

He drops a smoke grenade. The room explodes into chaos.

But while the Phantoms wage war across Auckland, Marcus "Sledge" Rawiri rides toward a different destination.

A warehouse in the industrial district. Abandoned. Isolated. The address Detective Morrison gave him.

He parks the Britten V1200 outside, its supercharged engine ticking as it cools. His hands shake. His heart pounds. He's about to betray everyone who ever trusted him.

For his family. Always for his family.

Sledge enters the warehouse. Detective Morrison waits inside, flanked by armed officers. But it's the figure behind her that makes Sledge's blood run cold.

Sara. His wife. Standing there with Aroha, Tama, and Kaia.

"Marcus!" Sara's relief is palpable. "Thank God you came. I thought... I thought you'd choose them over us."

Sledge stares at his family. His children look scared but safe. Sara looks desperate but hopeful. Detective Morrison looks victorious.

Behind them a squad truck awaits, the back doors wide open. As if the cops job was already completed, victory in hand, this being treated as mere formality. The special utility vehicle rear parcel tray 6x9 speakers. Also seemed to jester. Gloating obnoxiously as the radio bleared Billie Eillish songs "Bad Guy" and "Belly Ache". Purposeful or not this cut through Jesters subconscious like a hot knife through butter.

"Mr. Rawiri," Morrison says. "Thank you for making the right choice. Your family is safe. The Iron Tide is finished. And you..." She smiles. "You get to walk away from all of this."

"What do you need from me?" Sledge asks quietly.

"Uncle Dread's location. Real-time updates on the Phantom's positions. Everything you know about their operational structure." Morrison pulls out a recording device. "Start talking, and your family gets witness protection. Stay silent, and..." She looks at Aroha meaningfully.

Sledge's daughter. Seven years old. Clutching her mother's hand. Trusting her father to protect her.

He opens his mouth to speak...

...and Ghost's voice crackles over his helmet's comm system, forgotten in his pocket.

"Sledge, where are you? We need backup at Uncle Dread's position. The Serpents had a trap waiting. It's bad, brother. It's really bad."

Sledge closes his eyes. The weight of the world crushing him.

His family. Or his brothers.

His blood. Or his oath.

His children's future. Or his honour.

Detective Morrison watches him, waiting. Sara holds Aroha close, pleading with her eyes. And somewhere in the Auckland night, Uncle Dread and the Phantoms are fighting for their lives against overwhelming odds.

Marcus "Sledge" Rawiri reaches for his phone...

CHAPTER SEVEN: THE ORACLE'S GAMBIT

M*arcus "Sledge" Rawiri's hand trembles as he reaches for his phone. Detective Morrison's eyes track the movement like a hawk watching prey. Sara clutches Aroha tighter, hope and fear warring across her face.*

Ghost's voice crackles again through the forgotten comm unit: "Sledge! Uncle Dread is pinned down! They've got fucking drones and..."

The warehouse doors explode inward.

Not the police. Not Serpents.

Tommy "Jester" Finch rides his old trusty ZX10r through the entrance like a neon-green missile, flames shooting from the exhaust. Behind him, six more riders on machines that scream rebellion. A turbocharged Moto Guzzi Griso making sounds no Italian bike should make, two Yamaha FZR1000s rebuilt with modern electronics and oversized engines, an MV Agusta Brutale wearing carbon fiber like armor.

Jester kills his engine, the sudden silence deafening. He pulls off his half-mask, and his usual manic grin is gone. What remains is a cold calculation.

"Detective Morrison," Jester says pleasantly. "I believe you have something that doesn't belong to you."

Morrison's hand drops to her sidearm. "This is a law enforcement operation. Leave now or..."

"Or what?" Jester's voice drops to something dangerous. "You'll arrest me? I've got eight different lawyers on speed dial. You'll shoot me? My boys outside will level this building. You'll threaten the kids?" He looks at Aroha, Tama, and Kaia with unexpected gentleness. "That would make you the bad guy, wouldn't it?"

One of Morrison's officers moves. Jester's hand blurs to his Beretta, faster than thought. *"Don't."*

The officer freezes.

Jester walks forward, his boots echoing on concrete. *"See, here's what you don't understand about the Iron Tide, Detective. We're not just criminals. We're family. And family protects family. Even when..."* He glances at Sledge. *"Even when the family makes mistakes."*

"Marcus hasn't made a mistake," Sara says desperately. *"He's trying to save us!"*

"From what?" Jester's voice is soft now, almost kind. *"From Uncle Dread? From the Tide? Sara, do you know how many people have tried to leave the organization in forty years?"*

"How many?" Sara whispers.

"Seventy-three. You know how many succeeded?" Jester pauses. *"Two. And they only managed it because Uncle Dread let them go. Release them. Freed them."* He looks at Morrison. *"Witness protection doesn't mean shit when you're dealing with an empire that owns half the judges in this country."*

Morrison's jaw tightens. *"We can protect them."*

"Can you?" Jester pulls out his phone, activates the screen. *"Because according to the tracker we put in the Britten V1200, Uncle Dread has known Marcus's location for the last thirty minutes. He's known about this meeting. He's known about Sara's involvement with you. He knows everything."*

Sledge feels the world tilt. *"You... you were following me?"*

"Uncle Dread was following you," Jester corrects. *"I was just the babysitter. My orders were simple: if Marcus betrays us, eliminate the threat. If Marcus is being blackmailed, extract him."* Jester's eyes are sad now. *"I really hoped it was option two, brother."*

"My kids..."

"Are safe. They've always been safe. You think Uncle Dread would let anyone hurt them?" Jester laughs bitterly. *"He loves you, Marcus. He*

called you his son. That means something to the old man. That means everything."

Sara steps forward. *"If he loves Marcus so much, why won't he let us leave?"*

"Because leaving requires permission. And permission..." Jester's phone buzzes. *He reads the message, and something crosses his face. Fear.* "Ah, fuck."

"What?" Sledge demands.

"Oracle just made their move. The real move." Jester looks up, and his eyes are haunted. *"The Auckland Harbour Bridge. It's wired with explosives. Oracle's threatening to blow it unless Uncle Dread surrenders the entire organization."*

The warehouse falls silent.

"How many people are on that bridge?" Morrison asks quietly.

"At this hour? Maybe three hundred cars. A thousand people." Jester's voice is hollow. *"Oracle doesn't care. They want the Iron Tide, and they'll murder a thousand innocents to get it."*

Sledge makes his decision.

He turns to Sara, takes her face in his hands. "I love you. I love our kids more than anything in this world. But a thousand people are going to die if I don't stop this."

"Marcus..."

"Detective Morrison, you want to arrest someone? Arrest me. After this is over. But right now, I need to save those people." He looks at Jester. *"Where's Uncle Dread?"*

"Sky Tower. Oracle called him out for a meeting. Top floor, the observation deck."

"That's suicide. It's completely exposed."

"Yeah." Jester grins, and there's his madness again. *"But Uncle Dread doesn't do things halfway. He's making a statement."*

Sledge turns to his children. Aroha is crying. Tama looks confused. Kaia... Kaia looks at him with those fierce eyes and says, "Go save people, Dad. That's what heroes do."

Something breaks and heals simultaneously in Marcus Rawiri's chest. He kisses each of his children, embraces Sara one last time, and walks to the Britten V1200.

"Marcus!" *Morrison calls out.* "If you ride away from here, there's no witness protection. No immunity. No..."

"I know." *Sledge mounts the bike, and the supercharged V-twin roars to life like a caged god.* "But maybe some things are worth more than safety."

He launches into the Auckland night, the Britten's titanium frame singing with speed. Behind him, Jester and his crew follow, a formation of mechanical fury racing toward the city center.

Sara watches them go, clutching her children, and Detective Morrison lowers her weapon with a sigh.

"You just let your only leverage escape," *one of her officers says.*

Morrison watches the taillights disappear. "Maybe. Or maybe I just watched a man choose to be a hero instead of a coward."

CHAPTER EIGHT: THE SKY TOWER GAMBIT

The *Auckland Sky Tower* spears into the night like a needle threatening to puncture heaven itself. At 328 meters, it's the tallest structure in the Southern Hemisphere, a monument to ambition and excess.

Tonight, it's a chess board where gods play with human lives.

Ghost arrives first, his turbo Hayabusa sliding to a stop in the Sky Tower plaza. Armed police have cordoned off the area, but they part like water when they see the Iron Tide colours. Some because they're on the payroll. Others because they're terrified.

Apex materializes from the shadows, his H2R parked in an alley where cameras can't see. "Situation?"

"Oracle's inside. Top floor. Uncle Dread's on his way up via the emergency stairs. The elevators are rigged with explosives." Ghost checks his Glock. "This is a kill box. Oracle wants us all in one place."

"Then we don't all go in one place." Apex pulls out a tablet, showing thermal imaging of the building. "Oracle has at least twenty mercs inside. Ex-military, based on their positions and discipline. This isn't gang warfare anymore. This is professional."

"Who has that kind of money?"

"Someone with access to the Iron Tide's forty-two million dollars." Apex zooms in on the observation deck. "There. The thermal signature matches Uncle Dread. He's alone up there."

"Not alone." Ghost points to other signatures. "Dread, called his buddies too."

The sound of engines announces new arrivals. Sledge and Jester blast into the plaza, followed by six more riders. But these aren't Phantoms.

These are Iron Tide veterans, each one riding machines that scream personality and purpose.

A sixty-year-old ex-firefighter named Kane "Smoke" Barrett on a turbocharged Moto Guzzi California that he rebuilt in his garage. The bike sounds like a Harley breed with an Italian opera, all low-frequency thunder and high-rpm passion.

Two Māori brothers, Hemi and Rawiri "The Twins" Ngata, on matching Yamaha FZR1000s that they'd been modifying since the 1990s. Modern fuel injection, titanium internals, swingarms from newer bikes. They're not the fastest machines here, but they're reliable, proven, loved.

A former civil engineer named Victoria "Blueprint" Chen on an MV Agusta F4 that she'd specifically chosen for its perfect balance of speed and handling. She rides like she designs buildings, with precision and no wasted movement.

Bringing up the rear, a Samoan giant named Sione "Mountain" Tuilagi on a Suzuki Hayabusa that's been stretched, lowered, and fitted with a turbo the size of a toddler. The bike should be a drag racer, completely unusable on streets. Somehow, Sione makes it dance.

"That's everyone?" Ghost asks.

"That's everyone within thirty minutes," Jester confirms. "The rest are spread across the North Island, holding our positions against the Serpents."

"Serpents are the least of our problems now." Sledge dismounts from the Britten, his face grim. "Oracle's got the Harbour Bridge wired. A thousand people are hostages."

Ghost's face goes pale. "How long do we have?"

"Oracle gave Uncle Dread one hour. That was fifteen minutes ago."

Apex is already typing on his tablet. "I can access the bridge's traffic cameras, but I need someone physically on-site to assess the explosives. If they're on a deadman switch..."

"Then disarming them kills everyone." Ghost curses. "We need two teams. One for the bridge, one for the Sky Tower."

"No." Everyone turns to look at Victoria "Blueprint" Chen. She's forty-three, brilliant, and speaks so rarely that when she does, people listen. "Oracle is expecting us to split up. That's the trap. We all go into the Sky Tower, and the bridge explodes anyway. Some of us go to the bridge, and Oracle escapes with Uncle Dread as a hostage."

"So what do you suggest?" Sledge asks.

Victoria pulls out her own tablet, showing architectural diagrams of the Sky Tower. "I helped design the reinforcement work when they upgraded the structure in 2015. I know every access point, every structural weakness, every place you could hide an escape route." She points to the eastern side. "There's a maintenance shaft that runs parallel to the elevator system. Oracle's people won't be watching it because officially, it doesn't exist. Not anymore. We sealed it during the renovation."

"Can we unseal it?" Apex asks.

"I can unseal it in about three minutes with the right tools."

Ghost makes the call. "Apex, Victoria, you're with me. We go up through the maintenance shaft, hit Oracle's mercs from an unexpected angle. Sledge, Jester, you take the main elevators. Make noise, draw attention, be the obvious threat."

"What about the bridge?" Sione rumbles. His voice sounds like continental plates grinding.

"Kane, Hemi, Rawiri, that's your mission. Get to the Harbour Bridge, find those explosives, and figure out how to disarm them without triggering a deadman switch."

Kane "Smoke" Barrett cracks his knuckles. "Been disarming explosive situations my whole career. How different can it be?"

"These aren't building fires," Apex warns. "Military-grade charges, probably C4 or Semtex. If you're wrong, hundreds die."

"Then I won't be wrong." Kane's eyes are steel. "Fire and or sudden death doesn't scare me. And neither does Oracle! I will get this done, you can count on me"

They split up, engines screaming into the Auckland night.

The Auckland Harbour Bridge stretches across the Waitematoi Harbour like a steel spine, connecting the city center to the North Shore. Eight lanes of traffic flow across it constantly, commuters and trucks and tourists, none of them knowing they're driving over enough explosives to turn the entire structure into shrapnel.

Kane, Hemi, and Rawiri park their bikes at the southern approach. Police have begun closing lanes, directing traffic, but slowly. Too slowly. If they cause a panic, the stampede will be deadlier than the explosives.

"There." Hemi points to suspicious packages attached to the bridge's main support pillars. "That's where I'd place charges if I wanted maximum structural damage."

Rawiri nods. "Four pillars, four charges. Blow them simultaneously, and the entire center span collapses into the harbour waters below."

Kane approaches the nearest package carefully. It's a military-grade case, waterproof and impact-resistant. He opens it with practiced hands.

Inside: enough C4 to vapourize a city block, wired to a cellphone trigger.

"Remote detonation," Kane says quietly. "Oracle's got a phone somewhere with our lives in someone else's pocket."

"Can you disarm it?" Hemi asks.

"Maybe. But if Oracle's watching, they'll see me working and detonate early." Kane pulls out his own phone, texts furiously. "I need someone to jam the cellular signal. Block Oracle's ability to send the detonation command."

Rawiri is already on it. "I know a guy. Used to work for Spark Mobile. He can create a localized cellular dead zone, but it'll take him ten minutes to set up the equipment."

"We don't have ten minutes."

"Then I'll buy us time." Hemi pulls out a laptop, connects it to his phone. "If this is a cellphone trigger, it's sending a signal through a carrier network. I can flood that network with garbage data, slow everything down, make Oracle think it's just network congestion."

"That's brilliant," Kane says.

"Yeah, well, Rawiri and I didn't spend twenty years building computers for fun." Hemi's fingers fly across the keyboard. "Oracle's probably using a burner phone on the Vodafone network. If I can identify the specific phone's signature..." He trails off, concentration absolute.

Kane returns to the C4, studying the wiring. It's professional work. Clean, efficient, deadly. Whoever planted these knew exactly what they were doing.

"Got it!" Hemi shouts. "The signal's coming from... oh, shit."

"What?"

"The signal's coming from the Sky Tower."

The three men exchange looks.

"Oracle's watching from the same place they're threatening," Rawiri says slowly. "That's bold. Or insane."

"Or tactical." Kane stands, brushing off his knees. "They want to see Uncle Dread's face when the bridge explodes. They want to watch him break."

"So we don't let them." Hemi initiates the network flood. "Signal's have now been degraded. Oracle won't be able to detonate remotely for at least fifteen minutes."

"Then let's make those fifteen minutes count." Kane pulls out wire cutters and gets to work.

Inside the Sky Tower, Ghost, Apex, and Victoria move through the maintenance shaft like ghosts. The space is cramped, dark, and smells like rust and old fear. But it's unguarded, exactly as Victoria predicted.

"Three more floors," Victoria whispers. "Then we're at observation level."

They climb in silence, each one hyperaware that above them, Uncle Dread faces down Oracle alone. Every second counts.

Apex suddenly holds up a fist. Stop.

Ghost freezes. "What?"

"Motion sensors. Laser grid." Apex points to nearly invisible beams crisscrossing the shaft ahead. "Oracle's people aren't complete amateurs. They covered the maintenance access."

"Can we bypass it?" Victoria asks.

"Not without triggering alarms." Apex studies the pattern, his tactical mind calculating trajectories and timing. "But we don't need to bypass it. We just need to make Oracle's people think the breach is somewhere else."

He pulls out a small device, no bigger than a phone. "Sonic emitter. Produces sound at frequencies that make sensors think there's movement. I can set this off on the western side of the building, and all their attention shifts there."

"Then what?" Ghost asks.

"Then we move fast." Apex sets the device's timer. "Thirty seconds after this activates, we go through this grid. Victoria first, since you're smallest. Then Ghost. I'll bring up the rear and cover our exit."

Victoria swallows nervously. "I'm an engineer, not a soldier."

"Tonight, you're both." Ghost squeezes her shoulder. "You can do this."

The sonic emitter chirps once. Apex places it carefully, starts the countdown.

Thirty seconds.

Twenty-nine.

Twenty-eight.

Somewhere above them, Oracle is making demands. The bridge is wired. Uncle Dread's empire hangs by a thread.

Fifteen seconds.

Victoria positions herself at the laser grid, her body coiled like a spring.

Ten seconds.

Ghost and Apex ready their weapons. Whatever waits on the observation deck, it won't be friendly.

Five seconds.

Four.

Three.

Two.

One.

The sonic emitter screams, a sound like reality tearing. Shouts echo from above as Oracle's mercs respond to the false breach.

"NOW!" Apex roars.

Victoria launches through the laser grid with surprising agility, her engineer's understanding of spatial relationships letting her twist through gaps that seem too small. Ghost follows, his military training making the impossible look effortless.

Apex brings up the rear, and just as he clears the final beam, the maintenance shaft door above explodes open. Two mercs peer down, weapons raised.

Apex shoots them both before they can fire. The bodies tumble into the shaft, and Apex catches one before it hits the laser grid.

"Close," Ghost mutters.

"That's the job." Apex checks the dead mercs' equipment. "Body armor, comms gear, weapons. All high-end. Oracle's paying for quality."

They continue climbing. One more floor. Then the observation deck.

Then the reckoning.

Sledge and Jester stand in the Sky Tower lobby, surrounded by armed mercs. The elevators behind them ding pleasantly, completely at odds with the tension.

"So," Jester says conversationally, "anyone want to hear a joke?"

The mercs don't respond. Professional. Disciplined. Boring.

"Why did the criminal cross the road?" Jester continues. "Because Uncle Dread told him to, and you don't disobey Uncle Dread."

One of the mercs speaks into his radio. "We have two targets in the lobby. Instructions?"

Oracle's voice crackles back, distorted through electronics. "Send them up. Let's make this a family reunion."

The elevator doors open. Sledge and Jester exchange glances.

"You know this is a trap," Sledge says.

"Oh, absolutely." Jester grins. "But it's a fun trap. Those are the best kind."

They step into the elevator. The doors close. And they begin ascending toward whatever waits at the top of Auckland's tallest building.

The lift speakers were playing Bishop Briggs; River.

Sledge checks his shotgun. Seventeen shells. Not nearly enough.

"You think Uncle Dread's okay up there?" he asks quietly.

"Uncle Dread is always okay. He's Uncle Dread." But even Jester sounds uncertain. "Though if Oracle managed to take him hostage..."

"Then the Iron Tide falls tonight."

The elevator climbs. Floor after floor. The city spreads out below them through glass walls, millions of lights, millions of lives, all of them unaware that their world hangs in the balance.

"I'm sorry," Sledge says suddenly.

Jester looks at him. "For what?"

"For almost betraying everyone. For choosing my family over..."

"Marcus, shut up." Jester's voice is uncharacteristically serious. "You chose your kids. Any of us would do the same. Hell, I'd probably choose my Xbox over loyalty if it came down to it." He pauses. "Okay, that's a lie. I'd choose loyalty. But it'd be close."

Sledge manages a weak laugh.

"Here's the thing," Jester continues. "Oracle? Whoever they are? They knew your weakness was your family. They exploited it. That doesn't make you a traitor. That makes you human." He checks his weapons, the brass knuckles, the crossbow, the Beretta. "And being human? That's not a weakness, brother. That's what separates us from monsters like Oracle."

The elevator dings.

Level 60. The observation deck.

The doors open.

CHAPTER NINE: THE REVELATION

The observation deck is a circular room with floor-to-ceiling windows offering 360-degree views of Auckland. On a normal night, it's breathtaking. Tonight, it's a gladiatorial arena.

Uncle Dread stands in the center, hands empty, facing a figure in tactical gear and a full-face mask. Oracle. Around the perimeter, twenty mercs hold positions, weapons trained on the old man.

But Uncle Dread doesn't look afraid. He looks... amused.

"About time," he calls out as Sledge and Jester emerge from the elevator. "I was starting to think you'd gotten lost."

"We took the scenic route," Jester replies.

Oracle's voice crackles through a modulator. "The Phantoms, together again. How touching."

"Who are you?" Sledge demands.

"Does it matter?" Oracle gestures to the windows. "In forty-five minutes, the Harbour Bridge explodes. A thousand people die. The Iron Tide's reputation is destroyed. And I inherit everything the old man built."

"Inherit?" Uncle Dread laughs. "You think you can just take the Tide? You think forty years of blood and loyalty transfers because you planted some explosives?"

"I think the Council will follow whoever keeps them rich. I think the soldiers will follow whoever pays their salaries. And I think..." Oracle steps closer. "I think the age of Uncle Dread is over."

"Then you think wrong."

The voice comes from the maintenance shaft. Ghost emerges, followed by Apex and Victoria, weapons drawn.

Oracle's mercs spin, suddenly facing threats from multiple angles. The tactical situation has shifted.

"You were supposed to be dead," Oracle says, and for the first time, there's uncertainty in that modulated voice.

"Yeah, I get that a lot." Ghost moves to Uncle Dread's side. "Apex, you got that bridge situation handled?"

"Kane, Hemi, and Rawiri are on it. They've jammed the detonation signal."

Oracle's helmet tilts. "Jammed? Impossible. That signal is military-grade encryption."

"So are we." Apex's smile is cold. "You're not the only one with access to advanced technology."

The standoff stretches. Twenty mercs versus five Phantoms and Uncle Dread. The math doesn't favour the Iron Tide.

But then, math was never Uncle Dread's strong suit.

"Oracle," the old man says conversationally, "you made one critical mistake."

"And what's that?"

"You assumed I didn't know who you were." Uncle Dread's smile is terrible. "But I've known for weeks. Ever since the Prophet traced those financial transactions. Ever since Apex found the offshore accounts. Ever since I realized the one person with access to everything, who could coordinate with the Serpents, who could manipulate my people, was someone I trusted completely."

He takes a step forward.

"Richard 'The Baron' Branston. My oldest friend. My financier. My brother."

The observation deck falls silent.

Oracle...The Baron...reaches up and removes his helmet. Richard Branston's grandfatherly face stares back at them, and the warm smile is gone. What remains is cold ambition.

"Sixty years," The Baron says quietly. "Sixty years I've stood beside you, Dread. I've made you rich. I've cleaned your money. I've built your empire from the shadows while you took all the glory."

"You were always compensated..."

"COMPENSATED?" The Baron's voice cracks. "I made millions while you made billions! I stayed in the background while you became a legend! I did the hard work, the real work, and you... you got to be the king!"

Uncle Dread's face shows genuine sadness. "Richard. Brother. If you wanted more, you only had to ask."

"Ask?" The Baron laughs bitterly. "Men like you don't share power. You hoard it. You crush anyone who gets too close to your throne." He gestures to the Phantoms. "Look at them. Your 'sons.' Your 'family.' You were planning to give them the empire, weren't you? Four young men who've only been with the Tide for six years, and they get everything while I get nothing?"

"They earned it."

"BY BLEEDING? BY KILLING?" The Baron's composure cracks completely. "I've bled for you! I've killed for you! I've sacrificed everything, my marriage, my children, my soul, all for the Iron Tide! And you were going to give it away to these... these children!"

Sledge feels something twist in his chest. The Baron isn't wrong. In a horrible way, he's absolutely right.

"So you allied with the Serpents," Apex says. "You fed them intelligence, helped them plan their assault. You used Marcus's family as leverage. You stole forty-two million dollars. And for what? Revenge?"

"For justice." The Baron straightens, dignity returning. "I'm sixty-seven years old. I don't have another decade to wait for Dread to die and maybe, possibly, hopefully remember me in his will. So I took what was mine. And now..." He pulls out a phone. "Now I'm going to finish what I started."

"The bridge is jammed," Apex repeats. "You can't detonate."

"That bridge?" The Baron smiles. "That was never the real threat. That was just to get you all here, together, thinking you'd won." He types something on the phone. "The real explosives are in this building. Specifically, in the structural supports on floors twenty through thirty. When they blow, the entire top half of the Sky Tower collapses. Everyone up here dies. And the Iron Tide dies with them."

"You'll die too," Ghost points out.

"I'm sixty-seven and dying of pancreatic cancer. I have six months, maybe less." The Baron's smile is peaceful now. "At least this way, I'll be remembered. The man who killed Uncle Dread and destroyed the Iron Tide. That's a legacy."

Uncle Dread walks forward, ignoring the mercs' weapons. He moves until he's face to face with The Baron, close enough to embrace.

"Richard," he says softly, "I'm sorry. I'm sorry I made you feel invisible. I'm sorry I didn't see how much you were hurting. And I'm sorry..." His hand moves faster than anyone expected, grabbing The Baron's wrist and twisting. The phone clatters to the ground.

"I'm sorry, but I can't let you murder a thousand innocent people because you're angry with me."

The Baron tries to pull free, but Uncle Dread's grip is iron. For a moment, they struggle, two old men fighting over a phone and an empire and sixty years of complicated brotherhood.

Then The Baron laughs. "You think that's the only detonator? I planned for everything, Dread. I always plan for everything."

He bites down. Hard.

The suicide tooth hidden in his molar cracks, releasing its payload. Cyanide, fast-acting, lethal.

The Baron collapses. Uncle Dread catches him, lowering him gently to the floor.

"Richard. No. Don't..."

"Too late." The Baron's voice is already fading. "Eight Minutes. The charges blow. The tower falls. And finally..." He coughs blood. "Finally, I win."

He dies in Uncle Dread's arms, and for the first time in forty years, anyone sees the old crime lord cry.

"MOVE!" Apex roars. "Everyone out! Now!"

They sprint for the elevators, but one of The Baron's mercs, still loyal even in death, shoots out the control panel. The elevators freeze.

"Maintenance shaft!" Victoria shouts. "It's the only way!"

They run. Uncle Dread carries The Baron's body, refusing to leave his friend behind. The mercs don't try to stop them. Some actually stand paralyzed. None of them signed up to die in a collapsing building.

Seven Minutes.

They pile into the maintenance shaft, climbing down as fast as terror and adrenaline allow. Victoria leads, her engineer's knowledge of the building's layout their only advantage.

Six Minutes.

Ghost's ribs scream in protest. Sledge's hands slip on blood-slick metal. Jester cackles with manic energy, because of course he does.

Four Minutes.

"We're not going to make it," Apex states calmly. Always the tactician, even facing death.

"Yes, we are!" Victoria finds what she's looking for. An emergency exit that opens onto a restaurant balcony on floor forty. "Here! Out!"

They burst through the door into a restaurant full of terrified diners. Forty seconds.

"RUN!" Uncle Dread bellows, and the crowd scatters.

Thirty seconds.

The Phantoms and Uncle Dread sprint for the external fire escape.

Two seconds.

One.

The explosions start on floor twenty and cascade upward like a deadly waterfall. The Sky Tower's top forty floors shear away, twenty thousand tons of steel and glass and concrete falling toward the city below.

The Phantoms are on floor forty when the building starts to collapse. They feel the structure shift beneath them, the sickening lurch of a building dying.

"JUMP!" Ghost screams.

They leap from the fire escape just as the floor disappears beneath them. For a moment, they're flying, falling, dying in slow motion.

Then they hit the scaffolding of an adjacent building under construction. The impact is brutal, bone-jarring, potentially fatal. But scaffolding is designed to flex, to absorb force.

They tumble through multiple levels, catching themselves on support beams, grabbing desperately at anything that might slow their fall. Behind them, the top of the Sky Tower crashes into the plaza with a sound like the end of the world.

Dust and debris explode outward in a massive cloud that engulfs several city blocks.

And then, silence.

Ghost lies on a scaffolding platform twenty meters above street level, every part of his body screaming. Next to him, Apex groans. Above them, Sledge hangs from a beam by one hand, swearing creatively.

Jester dangles upside-down from a safety net, laughing hysterically. "THAT WAS AWESOME!"

"Jester," Ghost croaks, "shut the fuck up."

Uncle Dread climbs slowly out of the rubble, still clutching The Baron's body. He's bleeding from a dozen cuts, his face gray with dust and grief.

Victoria "Blueprint" Chen lies unconscious but breathing, cradled in a collapsed section of scaffolding that saved her life.

They're alive.

Impossibly, inexplicably, they're alive.

Emergency sirens wail across Auckland. Police, fire, ambulance. The entire city responds to what looks like a terrorist attack.

Ghost forces himself to sit up. His phone buzzes. A text from Kane "Smoke" Barrett:

The bridge is clear. All charges disarmed. What the hell happened at the Sky Tower?

Ghost types back with shaking hands: Oracle is dead. The Baron betrayed us. The tower collapsed. We survived. Barely.

Another text, this one from Sione "Mountain" Tuilagi:

Crimson Serpents are surrendering across the city. Word is their leadership is dead and their operations are burned. We won.

Won.

The word feels meaningless as Ghost looks at the ruins of the Sky Tower, at the emergency crews pulling bodies from rubble, at Uncle Dread crying over his dead friend.

Is this what winning looks like?

CHAPTER TEN: THE RECKONING'S AFTERMATH

Three days later

The warehouse in Greymouth serves as a temporary headquarters while the Iron Tide regroups. Outside, twenty-three motorcycles are parked in neat rows, each one representing a member who survived the Sky Tower and the war with the Serpents.

Inside, the surviving Council members gather around a folding table. Five of the original seven are left. The other two died when the Tower collapsed.

Uncle Dread sits at the head of the table, aged a decade in three days. The Baron's betrayal has wounded him in ways bullets never could.

"The Crimson Serpents are finished," Helena Bright reports. Her voice is subdued, traumatized. She'd been in the Tower too, had barely escaped. "Their leadership is dead or arrested. Their operations have been seized by police. Their remaining members have scattered or pledged loyalty to us."

"And our losses?" Uncle Dread asks quietly.

Matt Chen, the forestry operator, consults his notes. "Forty-two members died, across both islands. The Sky Tower collapse killed another thirty-three civilians, plus twelve of The Baron's mercenaries. Infrastructure damage is estimated at three hundred million dollars."

"Our parliamentary connections?"

"Intact, mostly. Minister Henyard is cooperating fully. The journal Ghost recovered is safely destroyed. The police investigation into the Tower is being managed."

Uncle Dread nods slowly. "And our assets? The forty-two million The Baron stole?"

Apex speaks up. "*The Prophet traced it to offshore accounts in the Cayman Islands. We've recovered thirty-eight million. The other four million are likely gone, but we're still looking.*"

"*Good.*" *Uncle Dread stands, and everyone falls silent.* "*I made a promise to the Phantoms. I told them if they helped me destroy the Serpents, they'd become partners in the Iron Tide. I intend to honor that promise.*"

He pulls out four envelopes, hands one to each Phantom.

Inside, legal documents. Deeds of ownership. Equal shares of the Iron Tide's legitimate holdings, worth hundreds of millions.

"*You're not soldiers anymore,*" *Uncle Dread says.* "*You're not enforcers. You're owners. You have a voice in every decision. You have the right to shape the future of this organization.*" *He pauses.* "*And you have the right to walk away, if that's what you choose.*"

The room holds its breath.

Ghost opens his envelope, stares at the documents. Enough wealth to retire twenty times over. Enough power to reshape New Zealand's underworld. Enough responsibility to crush a lesser man.

"*I need some air,*" *he says quietly, and walks outside.*

The others follow.

The four Phantoms stand among their motorcycles, each one still bearing scars from the battle. The turbo Hayabusa has a cracked fairing. The Britten V1200's carbon fiber shows stress fractures. The H2R's exhaust is scorched black. The ZX10R is somehow still intact, because chaos protects its own.

"*So,*" *Jester says eventually.* "*We're rich.*"

"*We were always paid well,*" *Apex counters.*

"*No, I mean rich rich. Like, never-work-again rich. Like, buy-an-island rich.*" *Jester laughs, but it sounds hollow.* "*Everything we wanted. Everything we fought for. And all it cost was...*" *He gestures vaguely at the ruins of their lives.*

Sledge hasn't opened his envelope. "*I can't do this anymore.*"

The others turn to look at him.

"Sara took the kids. They're in witness protection, somewhere I can't find them. Detective Morrison said it was voluntary, that Sara chose it, but..." His voice breaks. "My daughter's last words to me were 'go save people, Dad.' And I did. I saved a thousand people on that bridge. But I lost my family doing it."

"Marcus..." Ghost starts.

"No. Let me finish." Sledge takes a shuddering breath. "I've been thinking about what The Baron said. About how we sacrifice everything for the Tide. Our marriages, our children, our souls. And he was right. We give and give and give, and what do we get back? Money? Power? The privilege of watching everyone we love leave us?"

He holds up the envelope. "This is blood money. Every dollar represents someone who died, someone who suffered, someone who lost everything. The Baron. The civilians in the Tower. Tyler, my nephew. How many more people have to die before we admit that maybe, just maybe, we're not the good guys?"

"We're not good guys," Apex says flatly. "We never were. We're criminals. Enforcers. Killers. But we're criminals who protect our people, who maintain order, who keep worse things from filling the vacuum."

"That's what we tell ourselves." Sledge's laugh is bitter. "That's the lie that lets us sleep at night. But my seven-year-old daughter knows the truth. I'm not a protector. I'm a man who solves problems with violence. And she'll grow up knowing her father chose that life over her."

Ghost steps forward. "You didn't choose life over her. You chose to save a thousand innocent people. That's different."

"Is it? Because from where I'm standing, the result is the same. She's gone. They're all gone. And I'm here, holding a piece of paper that says I'm a king of criminals." Sledge crumples the envelope. "I don't want it. Any of it. I want my family back."

Silence falls over the group.

"So walk away," Jester says quietly. "Uncle Dread said we could. Take the money, disappear, find Sara and the kids somehow. Live a normal life."

"Can any of us live normal lives?" Sledge looks at each of them. "Ghost, you've killed how many people? Fifty? A hundred? You think that just goes away? Apex, you're a machine, but even machines break down. And Jester..." He smiles sadly. "Tommy, you use jokes to hide the fact that you're the most broken of all of us. How long before the laughter stops working?"

Jester's manic grin falters. For once, he has no comeback.

"The Baron was dying of cancer," Sledge continues. "He had six months to live, and he chose to spend it destroying everything he helped build. Because forty years in the shadows, forty years of loyalty and sacrifice, wasn't enough. It's never enough. The Tide takes and takes and takes until there's nothing left."

"So what are you saying?" Apex asks. "That we should disband the Iron Tide? Scatter and hope for the best?"

"I'm saying we should ask ourselves what we're really fighting for. Is it the empire? The money? The power? Or is it just because this is all we know how to do?"

Ghost sits down on his Hayabusa, and suddenly he looks exhausted. Not physically tired. Soul-tired. The kind of exhaustion that sleep can't fix.

"Afghanistan," he says suddenly. "Apex and I, we did two tours together. Helmand Province. You know what we told ourselves? That we were protecting democracy, fighting terrorism, making the world safer. Noble lies that helped us cope with the things we had to do."

He looks up at the stars beginning to appear in the Greymouth sky.

"But the truth is, we were just kids with guns following orders. And when we came home, when the civilian world didn't make sense anymore, the Iron Tide gave us new orders to follow. New enemies to fight. New noble lies to believe in."

"It's not the same," Apex objects.

"Isn't it? We're soldiers without a war, Vic. We're weapons looking for a target. And Uncle Dread gave us one: protect the empire, eliminate

threats, maintain the peace. But whose peace? The Tide's peace. The peace that lets supermarkets pay protection money. The peace that keeps politicians in line. The peace is built on fear and violence and blood."

Apex's jaw tightens. "You want to talk about blood? Fine. Let's talk about what happens if the Iron Tide falls. The Serpents were just the beginning. There are a dozen gangs waiting to fill the vacuum. Tridads, Hells Anglers, Comunches, Bandillos. Without the Tide maintaining order, New Zealand becomes a war zone. Is that better?"

"Maybe." Ghost's voice is soft but certain. "Maybe chaos is better than controlled oppression. Maybe people should be free to choose their own paths, even if those paths lead to violence. Because at least then it's their choice, not ours."

"That's idealistic bullshit," Apex snaps. "You've seen what happens when there's no structure, no control. Afghanistan, remember? Warlords and tribal violence and children stepping on IEDs. You want that here?"

"I want..." Ghost trails off. "I don't know what I want anymore."

Jester sits down next to him. The chaos merchant, the madman, the comic relief. But right now, Tommy Finch is just a tired man in his thirties who's seen too much and laughed to avoid crying.

"I had a sister," he says suddenly. Everyone turns to stare. Jester never talks about his past. Never. "Emily. She was three years older than me, and she was... she was everything good in the world. Smart, kind, funny without trying. She was going to be a doctor."

He pauses, and for the first time, his hands shake.

"She got caught in a gang shooting. Wrong place, wrong time. Stray bullet from a turf war in South Auckland. She was nineteen. I was sixteen." Jester's voice cracks. "After she died, I went looking for the gang that killed her. Not for justice. For revenge. I was going to murder every single one of them."

"What stopped you?" Sledge asks gently.

"Uncle Dread. He found me, gun in hand, standing outside their clubhouse. And you know what he said? He said, 'Killing them won't

bring her back. But building something that prevents other sisters from dying? That's how you honor her memory."

Jester looks up, and his eyes are wet.

"So I joined the Tide. I became a Phantom. And for six years, I told myself I was preventing violence, stopping turf wars, making Auckland safer. But Emily would be twenty-nine now. She'd be a doctor. She'd be saving lives. And what am I?" He laughs bitterly. "I'm the thing that killed her. Just wearing different colours."

The confession hangs in the air like smoke.

"We're all broken," Sledge says finally. "Every single one of us came to the Tide because we had nowhere else to go. Ghost and Apex from the military. Me from a dead-end bouncer job. Tommy from grief. We found purpose, brotherhood, meaning. But maybe..." He looks at the crumpled envelope in his hand. "Maybe we confused survival with purpose. Maybe we confused brotherhood with prison."

"So what do we do?" Apex asks, and for the first time, the tactical genius sounds lost.

Ghost stands. "We go back inside. We listen to what Uncle Dread has to say. And then..." He looks at each of his brothers. "Then we decide if the Iron Tide is worth saving. Or if it's time to let it fall."

They return to the warehouse to find Uncle Dread alone. The Council members have left, giving the old man privacy. He sits in front of a laptop, playing some of his favourite songs. Elvis Presley's top hits, You Ain't Nothin But A Hound Dog, Trouble and newer playlists consisting of Lucas Graham's 7 Years, Ed Sheeran's, I see Fire and Kaleo's On The Way Down We Go. Dread had another computer tab open, he was watching the news coverage of the Sky Tower collapse. The death toll has risen to forty-five civilians. Investigations are ongoing. Questions are being asked.

"The official story is a gas leak," Uncle Dread says without looking up. "Faulty maintenance, tragic accident. Our people in the police department and city council are managing the narrative. There won't be a criminal investigation into the Iron Tide's involvement."

"Because we own the investigators," Ghost says.

"Yes." Uncle Dread closes the laptop. "That's how empires work, Jackson. You buy the police, the politicians, the media. You control the narrative. You make sure your crimes never see daylight."

"The Baron understood that," Sledge says. "He understood the whole system. And he realized he was just another cog in your machine."

Uncle Dread's face tightens. "Richard was my friend. My brother. He was never just a cog."

"Then why did he feel that way?" Sledge presses. "Why did sixty years of loyalty end with him trying to kill everyone?"

"Because he was dying, angry, and irrational."

"Or because he was dying and finally telling the truth." Sledge steps forward. "Uncle, with respect, you promised us partnerships. Ownership. A voice in the future of the Tide. But is that real? Or is it another lie to keep us loyal?"

Uncle Dread stands slowly, and despite his age, despite his grief, he radiates power. "You think I'm lying to you?"

"I think you're used to controlling people. And I think you're very good at making people believe they have power while you keep it all yourself."

The old man studies Sledge for a long moment. Then, unexpectedly, he smiles.

"You're right."

The admission shocks everyone.

"I am a control freak," Uncle Dread continues. "I have been for forty years. I built the Iron Tide from nothing, unified the gangs, crushed my enemies, and created an empire. And empires require absolute control. One vision. One leader. One voice."

He walks to the window, looking out at the motorcycles lined up outside.

"But I'm eighty-three years old. I'm tired. And the Sky Tower taught me something." He turns back to face them. "Richard betrayed me because I made him invisible. I took his contributions for granted. I assumed his

loyalty was infinite. And he died hating me because I never saw him as an equal."

Uncle Dread's voice drops.

"I don't want to make that mistake with you four. You're not cogs. You're not even sons, really, though I called you that. You're..." He struggles for the word. *"You're the future. And the future can't be controlled. It can only be shaped."*

"What does that mean?" Apex asks.

"It means I'm stepping down."

Silence.

"As of tonight, I'm retiring. The Chatham Islands have been calling me home for years. I'm going to spend whatever time I have left watching the ocean and making peace with my ghosts." Uncle Dread pulls out four more envelopes. *"These contain my full shares of the Iron Tide. Split four ways. Between you."*

"You're giving us everything?" Ghost's voice is barely a whisper.

"I'm giving you the choice. You can keep the Iron Tide running as it is. You can disband it. You can transform it into something new. Whatever you decide, it's yours. No strings. No control. No puppet master in the Chathams pulling strings."

"Why?" Jester asks. *"Why give it up now?"*

Uncle Dread's eyes are distant. *"Because Richard was right. Empires built on fear eventually eat their founders. And I've been emperor long enough. Time to let someone else decide if this kingdom is worth saving."*

He walks to the door, then pauses.

"One more thing. Marcus, your family. Detective Morrison didn't put them in witness protection."

Sledge's heart stops. *"What?"*

"I did. They're safe, relocated to a town in the South Island, new identities, new lives. I made Morrison think it was her operation, but it was mine all along." Uncle Dread's smile is sad. *"I knew you'd choose them*

over us eventually. You're a good father. The Tide doesn't deserve good fathers."

"Where are they?"

"That's your choice too. I can tell you where they are. You can go to them, be with them, have the life you deserve. But if I tell you..." Uncle Dread's voice carries infinite weight. "You can never come back to the Tide. Ever. That's the price of normal life. Complete separation."

Sledge looks at the envelope in his hand. Billions of dollars in assets. Power. Control. Everything he thought he wanted.

Or his daughter's laugh. His son's dreams. His wife's love.

"Tell me where they are," Sledge says quietly.

Uncle Dread smiles. "Queenstown. 47 Gorge Road. Sara thinks she's there because of Morrison, but the house is paid for by an Iron Tide shell company. It's yours. No strings."

"Thank you."

"Don't thank me. Just... be happy, Marcus. Be the man your children think you are."

Uncle Dread leaves, and the four Phantoms are alone with their choices.

CHAPTER ELEVEN: NEW EMPIRES

T hree months after Waiheke Island.

The transformation of the Iron Tide wasn't just organizational, it was personal. With Uncle Dread retired to the Chatham Islands and the criminal empire restructuring into legitimate operations, the three remaining Phantoms divided the kingdom.

Each carved out their own domain. Each built something new from the ashes of what they'd been.

JESTER'S KINGDOM: East Auckland

The showroom gleams under LED lighting, three stories of chrome, carbon fiber, and pure mechanical poetry. "JESTER'S ASYLUM: Custom Motorcycles & Performance" reads the sign in neon green and electric blue, visible from the motorway.

Tommy "Jester" Finch stands in his flagship store, admiring his empire.

Forty-three custom builds are displayed across the main floor, each one a masterpiece of engineering excess. Triumph Speed Triples with supercharger kits that push 220 horsepower. Aprilia RSV4 1100 Factory's, wearing full titanium exhaust systems that cost more than most cars. Kawasaki Z1000s and Mv Augusta Brutale's rebuilt with turbocharged engines and electronics that border on AI. Suzuki GSX1400s transformed from sport-tourers into muscle bikes with attitude problems.

But Jester's pride and joy occupies the center of the showroom: a Honda CBR1000RR Fireblade fitted with a modified TVR Speed Six engine. Six cylinders, 4.0 liters, 450 horsepower, connected to a custom gearbox with a twin-chain final drive system that looks like it was designed by someone who hated the laws of physics.

"It's completely impractical," Jester tells a potential customer, a tech entrepreneur with more money than sense. "The power-to-weight ratio is obscene. The handling is twitchy. And the fuel consumption will make you cry. You'll spend more time at petrol stations than on the road."

"I'll take it," the customer says.

"Excellent choice!" Jester beams. "That'll be $385,000, and I'll throw in a free burial plot because you're definitely going to die on this thing."

The customer laughs nervously. Jester's not entirely joking.

Beyond the custom builds, the second floor houses Jester's personal collection. Mint-condition classics sealed behind bulletproof glass like museum pieces:

A 1998 Yamaha R1 in the original blue and white, the bike that redefined the liter-bike class. Only 3,400 kilometers on the odometer.

A YZF1000R Thunderace, the R1's predecessor, polished to mirror perfection.

A Kawasaki ZX-7R in Kawasaki racing green, from the era when 750cc was the superbike standard.

A 1994 Suzuki GSX-R750 SP, the limited edition with close-ratio gearbox and upgraded suspension. Worth more now than when it was new.

A 1992 GSX-R1100, the iconic "slingshot" Katana in cherry condition.

Three Honda CBR900RR Fireblades spanning different generations, showing the evolution of Honda's legendary sportbike.

And his crown jewel: a Honda CBR1100XX Super Blackbird, the bike that briefly held the production motorcycle top speed record at 312 kph. Completely stock, perfectly preserved, utterly illegal to ride at its full potential on New Zealand roads.

"You know most of these are worth more than houses," his business partner. A former Iron Tide accountant named Sophie Chang, points out. She handles the boring stuff: taxes, licenses, inventory. Jester handles the fun stuff: building impossible machines and convincing rich people to buy them.

"Yeah, but houses don't go 300 kilometers per hour," Jester responds. "Priorities, Sophie."

The Asylum isn't just one shop. Jester's expanded to six locations across the North Island: Auckland, Hamilton, Tauranga, Napier, Palmerston North, Wellington. Each one carries his signature style, organized chaos, high-end performance, and a complete disregard for what's "sensible."

His shops also employ thirty-two former Iron Tide members, guys who needed legitimate work and had mechanical skills. Jester pays well, offers benefits, and only has two rules: build quality machines, and don't steal from customers.

So far, it's working.

His phone buzzes. A text from Ghost: *Scorpions making noise. Need backup.*

Jester grins. The legitimate life is great, money's better, stress is lower, nobody's trying to kill him daily. But sometimes, he misses the simplicity of just shooting people who needed shooting.

"Sophie, I've got a business meeting. Hold down the fort."

"Business meeting" is code for "violence." Sophie knows this. She just sighs and returns to the spreadsheets.

Jester heads to the private garage behind the showroom where he keeps his own personalised arsenal. *His old nifty weapon the 2006 neon-green ZX10R, now fitted with an advanced Turbo and n.o.s systems, of course.* He also has a BMW S1000RR with every performance upgrade imaginable, a Buell 1125R (because supporting dead American brands is punk rock), and his latest acquisition. A Bimota Tesi 3D with hub-center steering that makes it handle like it's reading his mind.

He chooses the Bimota Tesi. It's fairly new, sophisticated and handles with precision.

Time to remind the Scorpions why the Iron Tide, even the new, legitimate version, isn't to be fucked with.

APEX'S DOMAIN: Central Auckland CBD

Victor "Apex" Drummond's office occupies the entire top floor of a glass and steel tower on Queen Street. The view stretches across Auckland's skyline, the harbor, and on clear days, all the way to Waiheke Island.

His company, "Apex Security Solutions," provides protection services to seventy percent of Auckland's major retailers, fifteen percent of Wellington's, and growing operations in Christchurch and Dunedin. What was once an extortion racket is now a legitimate security empire worth $340 million annually.

Apex sits behind a minimalist desk, reviewing threat assessments on multiple screens. His tactical mind, once used to plan assassinations and gang warfare, now coordinates security details, risk management, and crisis response.

It's still warfare. Just with lawyers and contracts instead of bullets and blood.

Usually.

His second-in-command, Kane "Smoke" Barrett, enters without knocking. "We've got a situation. The Scorpions hit three of our protected supermarkets in West Auckland. Smash-and-grabs. They're testing us."

"Response time?" Apex asks without looking up.

"Four minutes average. Our teams engaged, police arrived, Scorpions scattered. No casualties on our side. Two Scorpions arrested, three escaped."

"Not acceptable. Four minutes is too slow." Apex pulls up a tactical map. "The Scorpions are operating from Kingseat. Former factory district. They've established a base of operations there."

"Get Spooked?" Kane asks.

"The horror attraction, yes. Intelligence suggests they've taken it over, using it as a front for their operations." Apex stands, his six-foot-three frame radiating controlled menace. "I'm going to send a message."

"You want me to assemble a team?"

"No. I'll handle this personally. It's been three months since I've done field work. I'm getting soft."

Kane knows better than to argue. "What about the police? This is technically their jurisdiction."

"The police can arrive after we've resolved the situation." Apex pulls on his tactical jacket. Not gang colors. Professional black, the uniform of Apex Security Solutions. "Call Ghost and Jester. Tell them I need backup for a pest control operation."

"Pest control." Kane smiles. "I'll make the calls."

Apex heads to his private garage beneath the tower. Fifteen vehicles: armored SUVs for client transport, surveillance vans, response vehicles. And in the back corner, covered by a tarp, his H2R.

The Kawasaki Ninja H2R hasn't been ridden in three months. Apex removed the cover, and the matte-black machine gleamed like a weapon in the dim garage lighting. 310 horsepower, supercharged, track-only, completely illegal for street use.

Perfect for sending messages.

He mounts the bike, and for the first time in three months, Victor "Apex" Drummond isn't a CEO. He's a Phantom.

And Phantoms don't negotiate with gangs.

They eliminate them.

GHOST'S EMPIRE: North Shore & Beyond

Jackson "Ghost" Kowalski's transformation was the most unexpected.

He didn't open businesses. He didn't build security companies. Instead, Ghost took over the Iron Tide's most complex operation: the political network.

His organization, "Tide Advocacy Group," represents workers' unions, environmental groups, and community organizations. What was once blackmail and bribery is now legitimate lobbying. Ghost spends his days in Parliament, in council meetings, in negotiations with corporations and government agencies.

He's become what he never imagined: a political operator.

His office is modest, a converted villa in Devonport with harbor views. No glass towers, no showrooms. Just a small team of lawyers, policy advisors, and former Iron Tide members who discovered they were good at navigating bureaucracy.

"The Scorpions are moving," his assistant, Helena Bright. Formerly of the Council. Informs him, "They hit Apex's operations. Jester's getting the call-up."

Ghost sighs. He's dressed in a suit today, preparing for a meeting with the Minister of Conservation about DOC contracts. The legitimate kind, where they actually provide valuable services instead of just taking money.

"I suppose the suit won't survive what comes next," he mutters.

"Probably not," Helena agrees. "You want me to reschedule the Minister?"

"Yes. Tell him something came up. Emergency situation." Ghost removes his jacket, loosens his tie. "The Scorpions have been a problem for three months. Time to resolve it."

"Permanently?"

"Preferably without bodies this time. We're legitimate now, remember?"

"The police..."

"Won't move fast enough. The Scorpions are using Get Spooked as a base. That's civilian territory. If they're holding hostages or conducting operations there, every minute we wait puts innocent people at risk."

Helena nods. "I'll inform Apex you're en route."

Ghost heads to his garage, where the turbo Hayabusa waits. Like the other Phantoms, he hasn't ridden in months. The bike is dusty, neglected. But when he thumbs the starter, it roars to life immediately.

Some things don't forget.

Some things don't change.

Ghost Kowalski may be a political advocate now, a legitimate businessman, a reformed criminal. But underneath the suit and the meetings and the careful diplomacy?

He's still a Phantom.

And the Phantoms are about to ride again.

CHAPTER TWELVE: SHADOWS AND REVELATIONS

T**hree months after Waiheke Island**.

The transformation seemed complete, Ghost's political advocacy group navigated Parliament with unprecedented success. Jester's custom motorcycle empire sprawled across six locations, printing money with every turbocharged build. Apex's security company protected fifty-five percent of Auckland's retail sector, legitimacy wrapped around what was once pure extortion.

The Iron Tide had transformed. Evolved. Become something clean.

But evolution attracts predators.

JESTER'S ASYLUM - East Auckland, 11:47 PM

Tommy "Jester" Finch stood in his flagship showroom, admiring the Honda CBR1000RR Fireblade, his masterpiece of engineering excess. The bike represented everything the new Iron Tide aspired to be: powerful, beautiful, barely legal, but ultimately legitimate.

His phone buzzed. Ghost: *Scorpions making noise. Need backup.*

Jester grinned. Three months of legitimacy was long enough.

He headed to his private garage, mounted his CBR and rode into the Auckland night. Behind him, the showroom's lights reflected off chrome and carbon fiber, an empire built on speed and second chances.

APEX SECURITY SOLUTIONS - CBD, 11:52 PM

Victor "Apex" Drummond reviewed threat assessments across multiple screens when Kane "Smoke" Barrett entered his minimalist office.

"Scorpions hit three of our protected locations. They're testing us."

"Response time?" Apex asked without looking up.

"Four minutes average."

"Unacceptable." Apex stood, his tactical mind already three steps ahead. "They're operating from Kingseat. At the "Get Spooked" attraction. I'm going to send a message."

"You want a team?"

"No. Just the Phantoms."

Apex descended to his private garage, removed the cover from his H2R, and felt the transformation reverse. For three months, he'd been a CEO. Tonight, he was a weapon again.

Some things don't change. They just wait.

TIDE ADVOCACY GROUP

Devonport 11:58 PM

Jackson "Ghost" Kowalski was dressed for a ministerial meeting, he wore a suit with fancy square checkered tie and matching diamond shaped cuff links, the costume of legitimacy. Helena Bright came in and whispered in his ear, she informed him that the Scorpions were moving.

"They're using "Get Spooked" as a base. Holding hostages from the night cleaning crew."

Ghost removed his jacket, loosened his tie. "Reschedule the Minister. Tell him something came up."

"What about the police ?..." Helena quietly.

"Hmmm... you know the Red n Blue won't be able to move fast enough, the Phantoms will be too swift." Ghost headed to his garage where the turbo Hayabusa waited, dusty but ready. "Every minute we wait puts civilians at risk."

He thumbed the starter. The engine roared to life.

Some instincts don't fade. Some duties don't end.

Ghost was still a Phantom.

And the Phantoms were riding again.

GET SPOOKED

Kingseat, 12:34 AM

The abandoned factory complex loomed like a gothic nightmare. Three motorcycles converged from different directions: Ghost from the east, Apex from the north, Jester from the south west..

They regrouped in shadows three blocks away.

"Situation?" Ghost asked.

Apex displayed thermal imaging. "Thirty-two heat signatures. Twenty-eight clustered Scorpions. Four isolated in the main hall.....the hostages."

"Then we end this." Ghost checked his Glock. "No casualties unless absolutely necessary. We're the good guys now, remember?"

"Define necessary," Jester requested.

"If they're shooting at us."

"That's a pretty low bar."

They approached using tactics honed over six years: Apex mapped routes, Ghost took point, Jester provided chaos when needed. Three months of civilian life had dulled their edge, but some skills were muscle memory.

They breached Get Spooked's service entrance, dropped two sentries silently, and entered the horror attraction.

The interior was designed to terrorize: narrow corridors, sudden noises, disturbingly realistic gore. Tonight, real monsters had moved in.

They moved through the morgue scene, eliminating three more Scorpions, knocking them out cold, with no immediate signs of long term health damage present. Ghost's night vision picked up patterns, Apex calculated trajectories, Jester...well he accidentally activated the attraction's sound system at maximum volume.

Screams. Chainsaws. Demonic laughter echoing through the building.

"OOPS," Jester said.

Alarms blared. Red lights strobed. Gunfire erupted from multiple directions.

"SO MUCH FOR STEALTH!" Jester returned fire with his Beretta, laughing because the chaos felt like home.

They fought through twisted corridors of the haunted hospital, the demonic church, the serial killer's lair. Using the attraction's layout as a tactical advantage. Bodies dropped. Some Scorpions surrendered. Others fled.

They reached the main hall.

Four hostages, zip-tied and terrified. Six Scorpions guarding them. And in the center: Tommy Naera, the Scorpions' strategic commander.

"The Phantoms," Naera said, recognizing them. "I'm honored."

"Release the hostages," Ghost ordered. "Your operation is done."

"Is it?" Naera smiled. "See, I've been watching you three for months. The big transformation. The legitimate businesses. But you're not businessmen. You're killers. And killers don't change, they just find new excuses."

The words hit harder than bullets.

"You're here, surrounded by bodies you put down, proving the Iron Tide is exactly what it's always been: a criminal organization with better PR."

"He's not wrong," Jester muttered.

"Shut up, Tommy," Apex said.

Naera continued: "So here's my offer. Walk away. Leave the hostages. Or we execute them, and tomorrow's headlines read 'Reformed Gang Members Murder Civilians.' How's that for your transformation?"

Ghost's mind raced. Impossible position. Fight and lose legitimacy, risk the lives of the hostages and their positive new public identities, images, their new glowing national and international profiles. Or walk away, lose pride, lose face and their old underbelly true grit nature all together, that would mean surrendering, forfeiting. potentially leading to the Iron Tides merging,taking a knee,taking orders or running airin's for this **bastard**! and his **men**!

"We choose the third option," Apex said calmly. "We kill you so fast you don't have time to give the execution order."

"You're not that fast."

"Want to bet?" Jester's voice dropped to something predatory.

Tension stretched. Six guns on four hostages. Three Phantoms calculating trajectories.

Ghost made the call. "Jester. Left targets."

"Got 'em."

"Apex. Right and center, including Naera."

"Confirmed."

"I've got the hostages. On my mark. Three. Two..."

The lights died.

Complete darkness. The attraction's backup power failed simultaneously with every light source in the building.

Then a voice, amplified through the sound system...calm, educated, terrifyingly controlled:

"Gentlemen. How theatrical."

Emergency lights flickered on, bathing everything in blood-red illumination.

Standing in the main hall's entrance was a figure none of them expected: a man in his mid-thirties, wearing an expensive suit that seemed absurd in a horror attraction. His face was weathered but refined, bearing an unsettling resemblance to someone they all knew.

"Allow me to introduce myself," the man said, walking forward with absolute confidence. "My name is Frederick Dread. Though most people call me Fred. And before you reach for your weapons...look up."

They did.

Twenty figures occupied the catwalks above the main hall, all armed, all professional. Not Scorpions. Something else entirely.

"That's right," Fred continued. "The Scorpions were... let's call it a screening process. I needed to see if the Iron Tide's transformation was genuine or merely cosmetic." He smiled. "Congratulations. You passed. You're exactly as dangerous as my father said you'd be."

Ghost's blood ran cold. "*Your father?*"

"Oh, you didn't know?" Fred's smile widened. "Uncle Dread...my father...has been quite secretive about his personal life. Understandable, given his profession. But yes, I'm his son. Born to a woman in Kawakawa, raised between offshore islands all around New Zealand, educated at Oxford and MIT."

He walked closer, hands clasped behind his back like a professor delivering a lecture.

"My father built an empire in the shadows. Very impressive. Very... analog. But I've built something bigger. Something he doesn't even fully comprehend."

"What are you talking about?" Apex demanded.

"Power, Victor. Real power. Not extortion disguised as protection. Not blackmailed politicians. Not illegal operations laundered through shell companies." Fred, gestured grandly. "I own PowerCo New Zealand's controlling shares through a trust. I hold majority stakes in Auckland Transport and KiwiRail. My companies control forty percent of New Zealand's fiber optic infrastructure. And"...he paused for effect..."I own the rights to harvest and bottle water from seventeen of New Zealand's largest aquifers."

The implications crashed over them like a tsunami.

"Utilities," Ghost whispered. "Transportation. Internet. Water."

"The infrastructure of modern civilization," Fred confirmed. "Turn off the power to Auckland, and the city dies in three days. Shut down the rail network, and supply chains collapse. Kill the internet, and the economy screams. Restrict water access during a drought, and governments fall."

He smiled like a shark.

"My father spent forty years controlling criminal enterprises. I spent twenty years buying the systems that make civilization possible.

And now"...Fred spread his hands..."I own more of New Zealand than the Iron Tide ever did. Legally. Legitimately. Completely above board."

"Why are you telling us this?" Jester asked, his usual humour absent.

"Because I'm about to make you an offer. The same offer I made to my father three months ago, right before he 'retired' to the Chatham Islands."

The pieces clicked into place.

"You threatened him," Ghost said. "That's why he stepped down. That's why he was so eager for us to transform the Tide into something legitimate. He knew you were coming."

"Very good, Jackson." Fred nodded approvingly. "My father is many things, but he's not stupid. When I showed him what I'd built, when I explained that I could cripple the Iron Tide with a few phone calls and strategic blackouts. He finally understood the landscape had changed. Criminal organizations are obsolete in the modern age. Real power comes from owning the systems everyone depends on."

"So he stepped aside," Apex said slowly. "Let us transform the Tide. Give us both access to shared legitimacy and a united skeleton key to unlock everything."

"Because legitimacy and teamwork was the only way the Tide will survive what's coming," Fred finished. "A criminal organization I could destroy with government pressure, police action, legal warfare. But legitimate businesses? Those are harder to eliminate. My father was trying to save you by forcing you to evolve."

"And the offer?" Ghost asked.

Fred"s expression hardened. "Merge with me. Your security company, Apex, folds into my infrastructure protection division. Your motorcycle empire, Jester, becomes my premium transportation manufacturing arm. Your advocacy group, Ghost, represents my corporate interests in Parliament. The Iron Tide's remaining networks integrate into my systems."

"You want to absorb us," Ghost said.

"I want to offer you survival. I control the infrastructure. You control the enforcement and political capital. Together, we don't just rule New Zealand's underworld, we rule New Zealand. Period."

"And if we refuse?" Jester asked.

Fred's smile vanished. He folded his arms,now that ever they could see the resemblance between Fred and his father Dread. He then said "okay Now, I demonstrate what happens when you oppose someone who owns the power grid. Rolling blackouts across Auckland, unexplained technical failures. Your businesses collapse. Your political connections become worthless in the chaos. Your legitimate transformation becomes irrelevant when civilization itself starts failing."

He pulled out his phone. "I can start the demonstration right now, if you'd like. Auckland goes dark in thirty seconds. The blame falls on infrastructure failures. Nobody suspects corporate warfare. And by morning, your security contracts are cancelled, your showrooms are looted, and your advocacy group is screaming into the void while the city burns."

"You'd murder thousands," Ghost said.

"I'd create inconvenience. Big difference. Though yes, some people would die, accidents in the dark, medical equipment failures, traffic chaos. Acceptable losses."

Apex's hand moved toward his weapon.

"I wouldn't," Fred said calmly. Twenty red laser dots appeared on the Phantoms' chests from the catwalks above. "My people are former SAS, Delta Force, and Mossad. They don't miss."

The hostages whimpered. Tommy Naera and his Scorpions stood frozen, realizing they'd been pawns in a much larger game.

"So here's how this works," Fred continued. "You have seventy-two hours to decide. Merge with me, or watch your transformation burn. And before you think about calling my father for help"...his checky smile returned..."you should know: Uncle Dread hasn't answered his phone in three weeks. The Chatham Islands are lovely this time of year, but quite isolated. Cell service is unreliable. Accidents happen."

Ghost's stomach dropped. "What did you do?"

"Nothing yet. But I control the communications infrastructure, remember? One phone call, and the Chathams go dark. Another call, and supply boats stop arriving. My father is eighty-three years old. How long does he survive without power, communication, or food shipments?"

"You'd kill your own father," Jester said, horrified.

"I'd leverage him. There's a difference. He taught me that." Fred checked his watch. "Seventy-two hours, gentlemen. Think carefully. You can have partnership and power, or you can have principles and poverty. My father chose to step aside because he understood the future. I suggest you make the same choice."

He walked toward the exit, his security team maintaining their positions.

"Oh, and release the hostages. They've served their purpose. Consider it a gesture of good faith."

Fred Dread disappeared into the darkness, leaving the Phantoms surrounded by armed professionals, freed hostages, and the ruins of everything they thought they understood.

Thirty seconds later, the security team withdrew...melting into shadows like they'd never existed.

The Phantoms stood in the blood-red emergency lighting of Get Spooked, their weapons useless, their transformation meaningless, their empire hanging by a thread held by a man who owned the infrastructure of civilization itself.

"We need to reach Uncle Dread," Ghost said finally. "Now."

"He's not answering," Apex pulled out his phone. "I've been trying for two weeks. Assumed he wanted privacy."

"He's been cut off," Ghost realized. "Fred isolated him. Made sure we couldn't get advice or support from the one person who might know how to fight this."

"So what do we do?" Jester asked, and for the first time, he sounded genuinely scared.

Ghost looked at his brothers, the Phantoms who'd tried to transform, to evolve, to become something better than they were.

"We have seventy-two hours to figure out if the Iron Tide's transformation was real change or just a beautiful lie. Because if we merge with Fred, we become exactly what we were trying to escape. But if we fight him..."

He didn't finish. They all knew what happened if they fought someone who owned the power grid.

"Get the hostages to safety," Ghost ordered. "Then we ride. We need to convene everyone...Council members, operations heads, everyone who has a stake in what the Iron Tide has become."

"And then?" Apex asked.

"Then we decide if we're willing to become monsters again to fight a monster. Or if there's a third option nobody's seeing yet."

They evacuated the hostages, left the Scorpions to their fate, and rode into the Auckland night.

Behind them, Get Spooked's emergency lights flickered and died.

Ahead, seventy-two hours to save an empire.

And somewhere in the Chatham Islands, Uncle Dread sat in darkness, unable to warn them about the son who'd learned everything from him, and then surpassed him.

———◉———

THE END.

AUTHOR'S NOTE

To my family, friends, and readers who have embraced this story. This book exists because of the people who shaped me, challenged me, and believed in the power of stories long before I put pen to paper.

To my father, Frederick P. Barnes: You left us before you could hold this book in your hands, before you could see these pages that carry so much of what you taught me. You knew I was writing, heard fragments of these drafts, but never got to read the finished work or see your son become a published author. That absence sits heavy on my heart.

You were Vikings and Moriori, railway man and union negotiator, entrepreneur and storyteller. You never stopped moving, even approaching eighty. I never saw you sit still long enough for retirement. True grit, like Eddie "The Governor" McLean crossed with Billy Connolly's irreverent humor. You rode a Vincent Black Shadow you assembled from a box of parts, drove a '68 Ford Thunderbird, and maintained what you called a "spider-web" of connections spanning the country. This was all documented in your hand-scribed phone books.

Some of your closest family and friends called you by a nickname you earned in your youth, possibly in the mid fifties to late sixties although not many will believe this. We still have an old James Dean Picture, on the reverse side a faded personalised hand scribble reads, "to uncle Dreed". You might understand now why I chose the name Dread for one of the lead characters.

I did not want you rolling your eyes thinking I stole this from the British anthology Comic 2000 AD from 1977 or perhaps pinched or borrowed it from a Sylvester Stallone movie released in 1995.

The Phantoms' loyalty, Uncle Dread's complexity, the motorcycles that become extensions of their riders. These all carry echoes of you. This story is my inheritance from your life lived full-throttle.

I do hope the Valkyries came for you and your vintage rubber treaded charities of the past, and now you ride or drive united with your fallen comrades also previously from this plan or universe. Cruising together in the realms of Valhalla.

TO MY MOTHER LAURA Barnes: Through dawn-to-dusk shifts in prestigious kitchens, cooking for massive public events, you still made time to read me bedtime stories. You gave every character a distinct voice, paused for suspense even when the text didn't call for it, and made those worlds vivid enough that I could see them as my eyes drifted closed. R.L. Stine's *Goosebumps* and Stephen King's *Cujo*. You taught me that stories have rhythm, that words create worlds, that the space between what's written and what's imagined is where magic happens.

To my brother Mark: Your constant tinkering on two-wheeled machines. That Moto Guzzi Lario, Suzuki SV650, Triumph Speed Triple. Taught me that motorcycles are more than transportation. They're philosophy, personality, and purpose. The tips and tricks you shared while I worked on my FZR, GSXR, RGV, Thunder Ace, and ZX-10R became the technical foundation for the machines in these pages.

To Curtis the eldest and first of my half siblings to be born. who tragically passed before he reached retirement age. I imagine you have resurrected your classic Kawasaki ZX1100R. No doubt you are at top speed, still running from demons on the infinite highways of Hell.

Without my parents, brothers, friends, and the particular ways in which I was raised, these stories would read entirely differently. If they were written at all. Every character's loyalty, every mechanical detail, every moment where brotherhood matters more than survival. These came from watching how you all lived.

To my readers: Thank you for embracing my authentic voice, for accepting these flawed characters trying to transform without losing themselves, for understanding that stories about criminals can still ask questions about redemption.

The Iron Tide rides on.

———◉———

STAY TUNED FOR PART Two: The Pacific War